Comfort Food

Jo Hershberger

outskirts press

*"Food for the body is not enough.
There must be food for the soul."*

– Dorothy Day

To all the "Dorises" out there
(You know who you are)

And in memory of my parents,
Donald and Josephine Petry,
who taught me that growing up in a small town
might be the best thing that could ever happen to me.

Acknowledgments

I am indebted to the following people who provided valuable insight and information for this book: Ann Tudor, Martha Jeffers, Phil Buckmaster, Curt Campbell, LouAnn Williams, Katie Neuser, and Laura Pascual.

Prologue

September 2012

My name is Cherisse Lochschmidt, and I'm almost thirteen years old.

I haven't told anyone, but I'm worried about Grando. That's my Grandma Doris who owns The Boulder. I don't mean to brag, but it's the best restaurant in Rockwell.

The reason I'm worried about her is that she's worried about The Boulder and, like she says, "the whole damn town of Rockwell." I don't get it.

I know she thinks The Boulder's not as busy as it used to be. Too many folks are driving to Danville to shop at Walmart and eat at one of the new restaurants there. But they'll get tired of those places and come back for a piece of her pie. They always do.

I did hear her and Aunt Darcy saying some people at Midwest might lose their jobs if some of the stuff they do at the factory gets sent to a far-off place. Mexico, I think. But that hasn't happened yet, so everyone should feel good about that.

I sure wish Grando could feel good all the time 'cause when she does, she says whatever's on her mind. I know when she's grumpy it's 'cause her legs give her a lot of trouble, especially on rainy days. She got hurt and almost died in a boat accident when I was eight. She never complains, but you can tell by the way she sets her mouth that the pain is extra bad.

Other times she seems sad too. Grando had this bunch of friends that called themselves the Fearless Four that'd been tight since they were in seventh grade. About a year ago she was really shook up when she found out that the one named Kate had died of heart failure in her sleep. Her friend Rosie still lives in Kankakee but can't do much 'cause she has bad lungs and has to drag oxygen around everywhere she goes. The other one, Cheryl, is in Chicago. Grando says Cheryl is almost blind so they don't email anymore and it's hard to stay in touch.

I know Grando's slowed down a lot. She limps when her bad leg hurts but still thinks she's gotta go to The Boulder every day to make sure Aunt Darcy and my cousin Tiffany are "runnin' things right." Grando spends most of her time talking with the customers. Once in awhile though she still rolls out a pie crust or two, then we hear her sigh and say, "Times is changin'."

I hope Grando doesn't change too much. When she's feeling good she really rocks, and we love her the way she's always been.

Part I

2012

Monty

September

Montgomery Cooper was relieved to see that the morning fog shrouding the corn fields was lifting. For a moment—just a moment—he took his eyes off the road to glance at his cell.

"Deer!" Al barked from the passenger's seat.

Swerving, Monty glimpsed the startled eyes of a doe before it darted out of his path. As he steered his Beemer back onto the pavement, he realized that two fawns were following her. Again he hit the brakes. He veered to avoid the first one, then laid on his horn and jumped into the oncoming traffic lane to miss the second. Frightened but safe, the young deer ran back to his original spot. Monty's sweaty hands trembled as he guided his car back into his lane. A tractor pulling a corn picker lumbered past so close that he couldn't miss the farmer's one-finger salute.

"Damn. That was some fancy driving." Al's voice was full of admiration. "For a minute, I thought we were going to have venison for dinner." He chuckled at his own humor.

Monty cringed at Al's non-stop stream of inane patter. A week ago he'd been excited when his boss, Gordon Strunke, told him he'd be heading up a team to find a location for the company's new plant. He loved the challenges of being Director of Business Development for Goldstein, Riley & Nash and knew he'd gain valuable attention from upper management.

But he'd shuddered when he learned that Al Campanale would co-chair with him. Al was a loose cannon if there ever was one, and Monty dreaded the prospect of spending entire days with him until their project was completed. They'd received a list of five small Midwestern cities with an available work force and easy access for transporting materials, and told to submit an evaluation of each location by the following March. This visit to Danville, Illinois, was their first.

Monty admitted to himself that he looked forward to their short plane hops to the spots in eastern Nebraska and central Tennessee, but the thought of road trips like this with Al to Wisconsin and Indiana made him wish he could climb his company's executive chain a little faster. He also knew that his wife Claire wished the same thing. Lately, she'd devoted hours to poring over her stack of upscale real estate books and now had her eye on a prestigious property in Barrington.

"Man, I'm starving! Must've been the thought of venison." Al chortled again. His shirt already wrinkled, he squirmed in the creamy leather seat of Monty's BMW. "We've been on the road more'n two hours. Let's stop for something to eat before we get to Danville."

Monty bit his cheek in frustration. Hadn't he suggested they take I-57 from the Chicago area, then cut over to Danville? It would have been faster and they could have eaten at a Steak 'n Shake on the north side of town so they'd know what kind of food they'd get. Predictable, that's what.

But no, Al had insisted on taking state roads through Bakers Corners where a former girlfriend had lived. Who the hell did something like that on a business trip? Al, that's who. And he, Monty, had played Mr. Nice Guy the way he always did and subjected the BMW to canyon-deep potholes like it never encountered in the brick pavers at his private club back in Naperville. Now they were stuck in the middle of nowhere and Al was antsy.

"Can you believe these miles of uninterrupted farm-land?" Monty hoped if he diverted Al's attention from his hunger, the guy might stop complaining.

"Yeah." Al grudgingly shifted his gaze to the flat land-scape. "Makes you realize that food doesn't grow in cans. When I was a kid in Gary, I never questioned how all that stuff got on the grocery shelves. My dad worked in the mills. We hung out with union people. Not farmers."

"We didn't either. My hometown near Moline was about 20,000. Seems like a hundred years since I was there." Monty reflected on this realization as they passed a two-story house nestled amid a cluster of barns. "I guess I've never been in a farmhouse. Have you?"

"Hell, no. Don't plan to either."

"Can't imagine anyone wanting to live out here," Monty agreed. "No malls, no country clubs, no museums—"

"Hey—" Al sat up straight, "we passed a sign for a res-taurant. Let's get off the road and eat there. Our appointment isn't until 1:30 anyway."

"Catch the name of the place?" Monty hoped Al might see the folly of this back-roads travel route and suggest they head straight for Danville. And civilization. He tightened his grip on the wheel as his car bounced over squiggles of tar strips that laced the cracked pavement.

"Yeah. It said The Boulder in Rockwell has—get this— 'breakfast the way Mom used to make it.' Sounds good to me."

"Rockwell?" Monty could hear the disdain in his own voice.

"Well, it's bigger'n Bakers Corners." Al sounded like an enthusiastic ten-year-old. "C'mon. Let's put some fun into this trip. Turn left at the next blinker and go about a mile into town."

Monty sighed and eased the car around the corner to the left. "By the time we drive a mile, we'll be on the other side of town and out in the country again."

Passing several aging ranch homes in need of a coat of paint, Monty cursed under his breath. How had he allowed himself to get suckered into this wild goose chase?

"Up here, on the right. Past the video store. Blue sign." Al had put himself in charge. "There ya go. Into the parking lot. There's a spot next to that rusty black pickup."

Questioning how his orchestrated career path could have delivered him to the front of this nondescript building, Monty pulled between the faded stripes on the wavy asphalt. He turned off the radio in the middle of a Romney commercial and grabbed his suit coat from the back seat as he hurried to keep up with Al.

When he opened the door, Monty realized how hungry he was. The combined aromas of griddle cakes and bacon mingled with apple pie transported him back to the times he spent in his grandmother's kitchen.

"There's a seat over there." A server balancing four large plates nodded toward the window. "Be there in a minute," she called above the noise of the breakfast crowd.

Monty hoped he appeared cool as he gave her a quick thumbs-up and slid into the royal blue vinyl booth across from Al.

"Not bad." Al glanced around the room and fixed his eyes on the waitress. "Coffee for both."

He flashed the crooked grin Monty knew Al saved for girls he was trying to charm. "And bacon and eggs for me and—"

"I don't mean to interrupt, but I bet this is your first time at The Boulder, right?" Her blond ponytail swished as she returned Al's grin with a smile that indicated she was in charge. Monty chuckled.

"If you've never been here before, I'd suggest my grandma's French toast with a side of bacon. And," she paused, "a small dish of fruit, if you're doing the health thing."

"Sounds good," Monty replied. "Make it two."

"Hey," Al protested as the server headed for the kitchen, "we never even looked at the menus."

"Didn't think we needed to." Monty surveyed the room with its retro blue-and-white décor and its walls plastered with high-school basketball memorabilia. "We're getting 'breakfast the way Mom used to make it.' And" he added, "it doesn't include venison."

Doris

"I'll slide those pies in, Grando." Tiffany opened the door of The Boulder's aging but dependable oven. "You sit down and have a cup of coffee."

"Well, maybe." Doris considered her granddaughter's suggestion. "I've gotta check the meringue and turn the temperature back in a few minutes." She stepped out of the kitchen and into the dining room that felt more like home than home itself.

"When it comes to pie, you've got the magic touch," Tiffany reminded her. "Everyone in town knows that."

Doris savored the compliment, then waited while her granddaughter placed a mug of steaming coffee on the table of the back booth that everyone in town also knew was Doris's own.

She leaned on her cane, lowered herself onto the seat, and surveyed the Tuesday morning crowd. A perfect day, she thought—clear blue skies, a fresh nip in the air, and the leaves on the maple trees beginning to turn orange. Her early-bird regulars had finished their breakfasts and gone off to work. Now the mid-morning customers who had the luxury of lingering chatted as they enjoyed the breakfast special. Her gaze landed on two men in suits who were stuffing French toast and bacon into their mouths like they hadn't eaten in days. Obvious out-of-towners. After she looked at her pies, she'd go over and hope to trade a hearty welcome for all the information she could squeeze out of them. It was a bit of a trick, but she knew she had to try. You couldn't help but wonder why strangers had come to a town that didn't have a whole lot to offer anymore—not the way it had when she was growing up. At least Midwest Manufacturing, Rockwell's lifeblood, still was running most of its lines.

Doris drained her cup, returned to the kitchen, and peeked in the oven. Satisfied that the meringue had browned just right, she turned the temperature back so the pies could finish baking.

Threading her way through the tables, she stopped to ask one man about his ailing wife and another about his kid who was setting cross-country records before she reached the strangers.

"First time here? Then coffee's on us." She smiled, then winked. "But you'll still have to pay for breakfast."

"Well, thanks. Thanks a lot."

When she saw the serious one's blue eyes give her a quick once-over, she felt she owed him an explanation. "I own the place. I can do what I want."

"Best damn—'scuse me—darn French toast I ever ate." The younger, jumpier one with slick black hair mopped the last bite through a puddle of syrup. "You give out the recipe? I'd sure like my girlfriend to fix this."

She fingered her cane thoughtfully. "Nope, it's a secret.

But you can come back any time for more."

Inwardly she rejoiced when both men cleaned their plates and revealed they were from a western suburb of Chicago. Headed to Danville on a business trip, they said. She wanted to warn them what a godforsaken town it had become but thought better of it.

Before she returned to the kitchen, she knew the serious one had a wife and two teen-age kids and guessed from his body language he was strung pretty tight. She liked the one with the gift of gab better, maybe because he reminded her of a couple of her sons. He confided he'd been through two bad divorces but had a pretty cool girlfriend who was good company. She got his drift.

"Tell you what. If you come through here again, you let your server know that Doris said there's no charge for your coffee. You scribble your names on a napkin, and I'll know who you are."

"I'm Al. And he's Monty." The charmer pointed at the serious one. "Don't forget us—and we won't forget you, okay?"

"Got it." She used her cane to limp back to the kitchen. "Hot damn!" she congratulated herself. "I got all the news I wanted." A perfect morning and then some.

Helen

"If you don't get your act together, Haley, we'll be ordering hamburgers instead of brunch."

Helen Hamilton tapped her foot and glanced at her watch. As she waited in the high-ceilinged hall of their childhood home for her twin sister to put the finishing touches on her makeup, Helen sighed and wished she were back in her editing office in Manhattan. She admitted that her own years in New York City had heightened her impatience and that Haley's life as a specialist in serial marriage had given her a hard edge. Still, that's who her sister was now—Haley Hamilton Maxwell O'Brien Steinberg Champion—a woman with a string of last names. But that was all.

"Just chill, would you?"

She wondered how many times Haley's nasal voice had issued her solution for everything. "Chill."

A million, Helen estimated. And today was no different, although they were into their fifties and had returned to Rockwell to help their dad adjust to Happy Haven, the ironically named local nursing home. Because he'd never be able to live alone after his stroke, they had major decisions to make.

It wouldn't be easy, Helen knew. In fact, nothing had ever been easy where the two of them were concerned. Haley'd always been everybody's darling, the one who twirled the baton, dated all the cute boys, and didn't fuss when their mother insisted on bleaching her hair every six weeks. Helen, with her large lumpy figure, plain features, and hair the color of dead brown leaves, had won the county spelling bee in eighth grade but cringed with self-consciousness when she accepted the trophy. Now Haley jumped at the chance to use her real-estate experience to promote the sale of their dad's home as fast as possible. Helen felt they should take their time.

"God, Helen, Rockwell's turning into a nightmare." As they left the house and cruised past forlorn storefronts, Haley's words carried the same metallic quality as the old bandsaw their dad used for years in their garage. Wincing, Helen was grateful that at least her sister had the sense to hold her cigarette close to the open window. Their dad's aging Cadillac didn't need any more abuse.

"Black Beauty," as he always called his '75 deVille, had been their dad's pride and joy. With its ebony exterior and plush dove-colored leather seats, it held six people. When compact cars became all the rage, he rejoiced that he and their mom were the only ones left in their group who could haul two couples to the country club on Friday nights.

Helen tuned out her sister as Haley continued to spit out sarcastic comments about the number of consignment shops and abandoned retail spots downtown, the way she'd tried to forget the attention their mom had always lavished on Haley. If it hadn't been for their dad and his uncanny ability to encourage her when she needed it most, she would have felt like an orphan. She smiled at the memory of the day he took her—only her—to see the Cubs at Wrigley Field in August of '69 before the Mets had elbowed them out of a trip to the playoffs. She might be a New Yorker now, but she still hated the Mets.

"Cute guy." Haley cut short her monologue on property values to observe a short, black-haired man rolling a toothpick in his mouth as he approached a BMW in The Boulder's parking lot.

"Forget it. He's not from around here." Helen found a space close to the restaurant. "Rockwell folks don't wear coats and ties into The Boulder."

"Just sayin'." Haley stubbed out her cigarette in the ashtray. "No harm in looking for fun."

Ignoring her sister, Helen opened the restaurant's glass door and sighed. Every time she entered this place she felt as if she'd stepped back in time.

They found a booth and watched as the ponytailed server smiled and filled their coffee mugs. "Scrambled egg whites with whole wheat toast and a side of fresh fruit?" The waitress directed her question at Helen. "And one of those big cinnamon rolls for you," she added, nodding toward Haley.

"I'm impressed," Helen told her. "This is only the third morning we've been in, and you know what we want."

"That's my job. My grandma wouldn't have it any other way."

Haley's eyebrows arched as the girl scooped up the unused menus and headed for the kitchen. "Who the hell is Grandma?" she wondered.

"Mrs. Lochschmidt, the one who started this place." Helen sipped her coffee. "You probably remember her. Mother of Doug—and all the rest of them." Helen paused as she recalled her crush on their hunky blond classmate when he was the star of their high-school basketball team. But he'd always been draped all over that sexy cheerleader, Tonya somebody.

"Doug was cute, all right, but I was too involved with his buddy, Nick Rigoni, to try to snag him." Haley drummed her fingers on the Formica table. "Hey, is that the old grandma herself coming over here? With the cane?"

"Shh. Everyone can hear you." Wishing her sister could show some respect, Helen rose from the booth. "Mrs. Lochschmidt, Helen Hamilton." She held out her hand. "How good to see you."

"I thought that was you. Heard you was in town. Mind if I sit for a minute?" The older lady surveyed the space in the booth and slid in beside Haley without waiting for an answer. "Haven't seen the two of you together for years. And do call me Doris. You're old enough now."

When Haley shot her the look of an animal cornered by a predator, Helen realized she had to manage their conversation. She recapped her career that started one year after she'd graduated from college when Doris's brother, the famed pianist Tommy Panczyk, suggested she apply for an opening as a copy reader for *Arch* magazine.

"I don't know what I would have done without Tommy. He knew I was from Rockwell and used his connections to help me." She didn't add that she now was assistant editor and the publication's revered in-house grammar expert.

"Always knew you'd make somethin' of yourself." Helen felt Doris Lochschmidt's gaze sweep over her city haircut and classic tweed jacket. "And how about you, honey?"

"Oh, me. Not much new here." Haley squirmed and signaled for more coffee. "Been selling real estate in Florida."

"Married?" Doris's direct approach made Helen smile.

"Not now. Tried it four times though." Haley's voice softened.

"Kids?"

As Haley shook her head and studied the tabletop, Helen knew her sister wondered if Doris had heard about Haley's botched abortion their parents had tried to keep quiet during her senior year.

"Well, you always were a pretty thing." Doris placed her hand on Haley's. "But life sure takes some strange twists. I was sorry to hear about your dad. Me'n him were in the same class before I quit school to get married."

Helen could see her sister relax while Doris entertained them with detailed accounts of her own memories of Walt Hamilton. When Helen began to wonder how they were going to extract themselves from the situation, a slim fellow entered the restaurant and made a beeline for a rear booth. Helen thought he looked familiar but paler than death.

"Who's—" she started to ask.

"Pudge Simpkins. Oh my god, somethin's wrong. Awful wrong." Doris reached for her cane.

"Wait," Helen said. "How do you know?"

"He comes in about every day at this time with a joke for everybody. Always sits at the counter." Doris squinted in his direction. "Now look at him. He's all curled up in a back booth. Like he doesn't want to see a soul."

"I remember the Simpkins family—" Helen began.

"Nice talkin' to you," Doris called over her shoulder as she made her way to the back of the room.

"I thought she'd never leave." Haley let out a huge sigh. "I'm going down to Rigoni's to see who's hanging out at the bar."

"At this time of day?" Helen noticed the deep wrinkles etched around the edges of her sister's mouth, and how unsteady Haley seemed as she tottered on her pencil-slim legs.

"Never too early to look up old friends." Her twin gave her a slow, secretive smile.

Sighing, Helen collected her things and left a tip. She was fishing her credit card from her wallet at the cash register when she heard a wail from the back booth.

"Oh my god!" The voice was erupting from Doris. "Oh, my god!"

An eerie stillness followed. Doris, ashen and leaning on a table for support, faced those who stared at her.

"Bastards!" the owner of The Boulder shouted, pounding her cane on the tile floor. "Midwest's closin'. Screwin' us. Shuttin' down our plant!" Searching the faces of her stunned customers for any kind of explanation, she shook her head and crumpled into Pudge's booth. "Damn!"

Pudge

No bully—not even the grimy older guys at Sweet Briar—had ever punched the air out of him like his plant supervisor had only half an hour ago. Jiminy, Pudge marveled, it felt like a lifetime since he'd crammed into the lunch room with more than one-hundred-seventy other Midwest workers to hear Norris Nymquist. He'd reeled as the spindly head honcho cleared his voice and began to read the prepared announcement that fluttered in his hands:

"Management wants you to be the first to know that the operations of Midwest Manufacturing in Rockwell, Illinois, will cease on Friday, February 8, 2013. They will be merged with its newly acquired facility in Blytheville, Arkansas. Opportunities will be available for many of you who wish to move there. We will make every effort to help each of you find new locations of employment in this area. Any questions will be addressed by our corporate human resources officers who will be here on site for two hours next Monday. Thank you for your loyalty and service."

The eyes of Norris Nymquist darted about the room as

voices from the crowd pelted him with boos laced with profanity. He quickly collected his papers and scurried out the door.

"What the hell does all that gibberish mean?" asked one of Pudge's crew members.

"It means," growled another long-time worker whose grizzled face was set in stone, "they're shuttin' down, movin' to some hillbilly town in Arkansas, and we can't do a damn thing about it."

Pudge could only nod in agreement, worm his way through the crowd, and escape through the side door to the back lot. Climbing into his beloved ten-year-old pickup, he cradled his head in his hands before starting the engine.

He tried in vain to find answers to the questions that raced across his mind.

How could the people who ran Midwest—the place where he'd started as a janitor's helper in high school and scrapped his way up to line foreman—pull the rug out from under him?

What would he do now?

What could he do now?

What would Kristi say? His wife would hear about it right away in the school kitchen where she worked. He knew she'd be furious but would remind him they'd always lived within their means and didn't have a pile of credit-card debt. Still, it would break his heart to see the look on her face.

What would this do to Mason and Jenna? He sure hoped his kids wouldn't feel they had to quit their night classes and take on more work than they were already doing.

God. What should he do?

He glanced at his watch. Almost time for lunch. He could go home, but nobody was there. He could drive around and think. Shoot, he thought, that'd just waste gas. Automatically, he turned the key, pulled out of the lot, and drove toward The Boulder.

There he took comfort from the aroma of pancakes, bacon, and strong black coffee, even though he was a soda man himself. Ignoring the greetings of "Hey, Pudge" from lunch buddies at the counter, he headed straight toward an empty back booth where he could sort out his feelings. He nodded toward Tiffany, who would bring him his ham salad on white with chips and a bottle of cream soda as if nothing had gone wrong that morning.

But when his order arrived, he could only stare at it. Lightheaded, he sipped at his drink and gazed into space.

"You okay, Pudge? You're not in your regular spot." Doris Lochschmidt put her weight on her cane and peered at him. "You look a little peaked."

"I got bad news, Miss D," he said, using his pet name for her. "Midwest is shuttin' down." His whispered words, like poisonous fumes, hung in the air.

"What?" She leaned closer.

When he repeated himself, she howled and wobbled on her cane. Afraid she was going to pass out, he jumped up and offered his arm for support as she collapsed into his booth.

"Can't be," she groaned.

"Is."

"But—"

"I know."

As they stared at each other in shared misery, he watched

a large tear carve a path through the powder that covered her withered cheeks.

"Oh my god!" she shouted.

"Mom! You need help?" Darcy came running from the kitchen.

"Bastards!" She pounded her cane on the floor.

"Grandma!" Tiffany dropped a stack of menus onto a nearby table and joined them.

Miss D smiled weakly at her daughter and granddaughter. "I'm okay." She took a deep breath. "Pudge here says Midwest's shuttin' down."

"No way!" Tiffany's voice was full of disbelief.

"Oh my god, no!" Darcy's face flushed.

"Oh my god, yes." Miss D said. "It's gonna hit all of us. But you, Pudge—" she couldn't finish.

Touched by her sympathy, he felt the initial shock begin to fade and the chill of cold reality creep over him.

"It's gonna be bad. Real bad." He fixed his eyes on his sandwich and felt his stomach lurch. "I think—I think I'd better get a box for my lunch."

Cherisse

"Grando! Your finger's bleeding." Startled by the sight of blood on the chopping board, Cherisse dropped her backpack on the counter and grabbed a wet cloth.

"Here," she instructed her grandmother. "Hold this against it tight. That's what my mom tells me to do."

"Damn knife slipped while I was cuttin' carrots."

Cherisse studied her grandmother. It wasn't like Grando to have a shaky hand.

"You okay?"

"Will be," Grando grumbled. "Now we'll have to sterilize that board and throw out the bloody carrots. Damn Midwest."

"Midwest? What do they have to do with the carrots?" This day had turned way too weird, Cherisse thought. First, she'd heard at school that the factory was closing, and now she found Grando in a nasty mood with a bloody finger. She always looked forward to stopping in after school to fill the salt and pepper shakers and set the tables for the supper crowd, but today everything seemed off.

"You hear they're shuttin' down?"

Cherisse nodded as she heard Grando cuss under her breath.

"Can't believe they'd do that to us." Grando peeked under the cloth, scowled, and re-wrapped her finger. Cherisse could almost see the anger pouring out of her grandmother like the hornets from the nest she'd poked with a stick when she was four. "You know my own mother worked half her life at that place to put food on our table."

"Uh huh." She unscrewed the lids on the salt and pepper shakers lined up on a tray. "And Uncle Charley too, right?"

"You bet. My brother could've had his pick of jobs anywhere in the country when he finished college. But he came back here to join the management team. Did you know he ran the whole place for a long time?"

"Yep." Cherisse couldn't count the number of times she'd heard the Uncle Charley stories. She knew he'd been a star basketball player and one of the most successful men in Rockwell, but she wasn't about to interrupt Grando. Instead, she began to fill the shakers and let her grandmother ramble.

"Thank God your cousin Mallory didn't go to work there when Charley offered her a job on the line." Cherisse watched as Grando checked her finger again. "If she hadn't stuck to her guns and taken those studies to be a dentist's helper when she got out of high school, her and Ryan and the kids would be up shit creek right now. Oops. Sorry."

"And you and her both would be nervous wrecks." Cherisse ignored Grando's language as she switched her thoughts to cousin Tiffany's sister, Mallory. A few years ago, when Grando had finished her rehab after the boat accident,

Mallory and her new husband had moved in with her to help. Now they and the three kids they'd added—Cory, four, and his two-year-old twin sisters Annette ("Nettie") and Emily ("Emmy")—were still living with Grando. "Mallory could've worked here though, right?"

"Not on your life," Grando fished out a bandage from a drawer and began to unwrap it. "Back when she was in high school and Tiffany was already helpin' out here, their mom told me not to hire her. Said the two sisters got along part of the time but there was trouble when they worked together."

"Aunt Darcy told you that?" Cherisse screwed the top on the last pepper shaker. She couldn't imagine her aunt suggesting that quirky, fun-loving Mallory should not have a job at The Boulder.

"Hard to believe, I know. But that's how it is in families." Grando applied the bandage and flexed her hand. "Relatives can get their noses out of joint over the tiniest thing. You've been spared that, you know? Bein' an only child and all."

She tried to digest what Grando was telling her. After all, if you were any part of Grando's rambling family, you never felt like an only child.

Cherisse had pieced together bits of her life story since she was old enough to realize her relatives were talking about her when they thought she wasn't listening. Her "wild-and-crazy" mom had a fling with a drug salesman when she was in high school but couldn't stand the thought of being tied down with the baby girl she had a few months later. More often than not, Cherisse's Grandpa Doug took care of her while her mom partied in the taverns south of Danville.

By the time she was six, her birth mother had run off to

Arizona with a guy and never returned. After Grandpa Doug married the kindergarten teacher, Maria Malone, the two of them stepped up big-time. Cherisse secretly thought that the day they adopted her and she started calling them "Daddio" and "Matka," (which Grando said was Polish for "mama") was the luckiest day of her whole life.

"It's all worked out for the best for me 'n you. You've got Dougie and Maria, and I love havin' Mallory and her family livin' with me. You know me. I'd take noise over dead quiet any day." She paused to correct herself. "Well, <u>almost</u> any day."

She brought out a clean chopping board and began cutting carrots with a little more respect. "Hey, do me a favor and check the back room to make sure we have plenty of cream soda. Don't want to disappoint Pudge."

"Why do they call him Pudge?" Cherisse was relieved to have Grando's thoughts drift onto something other than Midwest. "I mean he's, like, so skinny and all."

For the first time that afternoon, Grando chuckled.

"When he was a baby he was a real butterball. Dougie saw him when he was about a year old and said if you put him on top of the hill out on McLaughlin's farm, he'd roll right down. Cute as all get-out but fat as could be. His folks called him Pudgey."

"What happened?" Cherisse asked. "Did he get real sick or something?"

"Nope." Grando surveyed her pile of carrots and decided to cut up a few more. "He started walkin' is what he did. Runnin' was more like it. He was the youngest of all nine of them Simpkins kids, and no one could keep up with him."

Grando smiled as she remembered. "Ran that fat right off. But you know what?"

"What?" She was glad to see Grando emerging from her funk.

"They still called him Pudgey, then Pudge as he got older. Funny name for a guy who hasn't got an extra ounce of fat on him."

"Maybe you oughta give him a slice of your pie when he comes in."

"Maybe I should, kiddo. Maybe I should." Cherisse basked in the warmth of the moment as Grando's eyes rested lovingly on her. "Now me'n you had better get to work or we won't be ready for the supper crowd."

Cherisse turned to hide her smile. Neither had mentioned that they might not have a crowd for supper that night.

Monty

B ack in his BMW, Monty made an executive decision to take the interstate home from Danville. He'd planned to discuss the pros and cons of the site they toured, but Al was snoring before they reached the city limits.

Grateful for the moments of silence, Monty used the time to take stock of his own career that had advanced nicely since he joined the firm two years out of college. He hoped someday his own vision and hard work would propel him into the tiny circle of rising stars senior management considered for major promotions.

He scowled at the long row of orange barrels ahead that threatened to make him late for his meeting tonight. Relieved to find the construction area was only three miles long, he switched on the cruise control and reflected on the guts and ingenuity the three founders of GRN had used to propel their small neighborhood grocery store into an international firm.

Every company employee could recite the tale of how World War II Marine vets Lou Goldstein, Dennis Reilly, and Jerry Norton had taken a flying leap in 1946 and opened a market in Oak Park, a suburban community that bordered the western edge of Chicago. After six weeks they added two female employees to double as check-out girls, shelf stockers, and potato-salad assistants.

Two years later the partners added a larger store in Naperville, then a third in Elmhurst. When Goldstein suggested on their fifth anniversary that they buy stock in an area cannery, the other two balked and the trio almost went separate ways. But Goldstein prevailed and had always been on the lookout for similar opportunities to help GRN expand.

Today, the company was on the leading edge of the booming natural foods industry. Monty hoped he and Al could recommend the best location for the new plant. After all, the people at GRN were excited about this facility that would produce natural fruit enhancements to replace artificial chemicals in foods ranging from yogurts to baked goods.

They'd have to talk about Danville as a possibility at the office the next day, Monty realized. When Al wakened in the middle of a traffic jam on the Tri-State, he was too groggy to hold an intelligent conversation. Monty guided the BMW between semis and SUVs to reach their exit, then deposited Al at his car in front of their office. He zipped down side streets to stick to his evening schedule and felt grateful when his two-story brick home came into view.

"You're running late, Monty," Claire called from the kitchen. "Fifteen minutes. I've been holding dinner."

"Seventeen." He kissed the back of her neck as she placed cartons of Chinese food next to the stack of square plates she'd bought last month at Crate & Barrel. "I'm lucky I'm home now. Except for one spot, we made decent time on I-57. Then we hit the Tri-State. I would've called, but it was a nightmare out there."

"Traffic bad on the way down?"

Monty could tell from her tone she wasn't interested but felt she needed to ask.

"Not the way we went. Took some state roads and had a late breakfast in a diner off the beaten path. I'll tell you about it sometime."

"Right. Sometime." She left the kitchen and called upstairs. "Theo. Cass. Dinner's on. Last one here does the dishes."

Claire really knew how to motivate their kids, he thought as he watched their thirteen-year-old daughter elbow her way ahead of her fifteen-year-old brother.

"Ha!" Cassidy announced triumphantly as she hopped onto a stool at their breakfast bar and ladled a heaping portion of white rice onto her plate. "Beat ya!"

"Just 'cause you act like you're still on the basketball court." Calmly Theo peered into one carton, passed it to his mother, and opted for the sesame chicken. Monty marveled at the way his son sidestepped Cassidy's head-on confrontations. If Theo could learn how to maneuver as deftly on the basketball court, he might become a better player than his sturdy sister.

First, though, he'd need to put some meat on his bones. Monty hadn't liked the way a novice sportswriter for the local paper described Theo in the pre-season write-up for the freshman team. "Willowy," the guy tagged him. Not a "tough string bean," as Monty would have preferred, but "willowy." What the hell did that mean?

"Slide that shrimp stuff down my way," he told his son.

"I've got to be at the 'Y' in twenty minutes."

"And I'm going to meet with my dance board." Claire kept her eyes on her plate. "Gabriella's announcing the cast for *The Nutcracker* tonight. I hope they have good news for you, Theo."

"Who the hell is Gab—?" He hated it when his wife threw him a curve—especially on a busy evening.

"You know." Claire's tone sounded as if she were addressing a four-year-old. "She's the artistic director."

Monty felt the last thing his son needed was a dance dodo named Gabriella. "How can the kid move up on the basketball team if he's practicing some dance thing?"

"Monty, you don't practice ballet. You <u>rehearse</u> it." His wife's answer was patronizing. "He was asked to audition for the part of the young prince last week, and from what I hear he did a very nice job."

"God!" No longer hungry, he let his fork fall to his plate. "I'd sure like to be kept up on the news in my own family." Glancing at his watch, he realized he didn't have time for a full-blown argument.

Claire flashed a demure smile and continued eating. As he stomped down the hall and grabbed his windbreaker, Monty heard Cassidy start in on her brother.

"You ate two egg rolls! Hog! Did you really eat two?"

In the silence that followed, he imagined Theo's shrug as he poked at his food.

"Jerk!" Cassidy's disgusted jab was the last word he heard as he closed the door behind him. Outside, the tip of a harvest moon peeked over the maple woods to the east. Monty allowed himself a moment to let the crisp fall air fill his lungs before he took the wheel of his Beemer again. He was right on time and couldn't wait to start the planning session with his "Y" board to set up a committee to help boys and girls who needed guidance and companionship.

His meeting ended on schedule, but by the time he reached home, Claire was asleep—or at least pretended to be. He checked his email and the next day's calendar, then tumbled into bed. When the alarm went off at 5:30, he dressed, picked up the hard-boiled egg and fruit cup he'd eat at his desk, and was on the way to his gym in twenty minutes.

People accused him of being driven, he mused as he skimmed through his usual routine in the lap pool. They had no idea how carefully he carved up the minutes of his life to accomplish so much. His office walls at work were lined with awards he'd received for his contributions to the "Y," Little League, and the Community Pantry he supervised.

He choked on some water as he made a turn. At forty-two, he was on track to be a top officer at GRN before his fiftieth birthday and was admired as an excellent father and husband. Well, he admitted, Claire might give him a "C" on that last category.

Lately, he'd grown resentful of the social events she scheduled for them. People he didn't know and didn't care to know held parties she insisted they attend because it would help their family achieve more prominence. His dad would've told Monty that Claire was a "goddamned social climber," but unfortunately "Ol' Ted," a retired bricklayer, now endured empty days in a nursing home near Moline, crushed by the fact his crippling arthritis and heart failure made it impossible for him to haul catfish out of the Mississippi anymore.

Monty climbed out of the pool, toweled off, and strode toward the locker room. Invigorated by his workout, he stopped to check his physique in the mirror. Still six-foot-two inches, he maintained most of the muscle tone he had when he played basketball for Northwestern. His brown hair showed fewer gray flecks than most of the guys his age, but he didn't like the new wrinkles that seemed to appear daily on his forehead.

At work, he and Al compiled a positive report on their research in Danville and agreed they needed to give the location a second look after they'd finished their other assigned trips. Grateful that his secretary's efficiency allowed him to make the most of his day, he hoped Claire would have dinner ready so he could eat quickly before Theo's game.

On the way home, Monty reminded himself he needed to make the time to teach his son the art of passing the ball. Maybe then Theo wouldn't appear as awkward as he had during the two minutes he played in the first game. "Willowy." God, he thought, what a terrible adjective to use on a guy!

The house seemed oddly quiet when he shut the back door. As he inhaled the familiar aroma of pizza, Monty puzzled over the fact that Theo's coat dangled from a hook in the back hall. The kid should be grabbing a bite and warming up with the rest of the team. When Claire appeared in the kitchen doorway wearing a brittle smile, he realized something was amiss.

"Cass will be home in a few minutes, so I tossed in a frozen pizza for dinner," she said. "Salad's already made."

"Hope it's Giordano's." He found a bottle of water in the fridge and opened it. "We should have plenty of time to get to Theo's game." He turned toward the family room when Claire's voice stopped him.

"We don't need to go tonight, Cooper."

"Wha—?" The fact she'd called him "Cooper" rather than "Monty" was a warning signal. She always did that when she needed to emphasize how serious she was about an issue. Still, under her impeccable makeup, she radiated excitement.

"Theo won't be playing."

"Won't be . . .? God, did he get hurt at practice? Or sick?" Something bad had happened to his son. He knew it.

"Neither." Claire broke into a broad smile. "Theo quit the team today. He's going to play the young prince in *The Nutcracker.*"

He felt his world begin to tilt. Quit the team? How could he? Monty had nurtured the dream they had shared: Theo would follow in his father's footsteps at Northwestern. But only if Theo worked hard enough, he'd warned him. God, the kid hadn't practiced in the driveway lately, Monty realized. But play a role in a ballet? God! Not his son!

"That young man and I are having a talk." He galloped up the stairs two at a time to Theo's bedroom. Once he reached the door, Monty took a deep breath. He'd show the kid what a mistake he'd made.

"Hey, Theo," he called. "Okay if we talk?"

"Sure."

Monty's heart lurched as he saw his son sprawled on the bed, his tousled blond hair framing a face blessed with Claire's Scandinavian cheekbones. The room—how long had it been since he'd been inside it—had changed. A symphony orchestra filled Theo's space with Tchaikovsky. Pictures of two ballet stars now covered the walls once blanketed with sports posters.

"Your mom says no basketball tonight." Monty remained standing as he played his first conversational card.

"Right." Theo didn't look away. His blue eyes met Monty's.

"You feel okay? Pull a muscle? Hurt a knee?" He wanted to make sure his son was all right.

"Yep, I feel fine. Nope, I'm not hurt."

"Then what—? Why—?"

"Dad, I got a big break today. They want me to dance the part of the young prince in *The Nutcracker.*" Theo's eyes glowed as his words spilled out. "I won't have time for both. Can't do basketball and dance too."

"But Theo." He groped for the right words. "You'll never play at Northwestern if you don't stay with it. Your future—"

"I don't give a shit about playing for Northwestern."

His son's proclamation cut him to the core. This had been their goal. Throughout Theo's childhood they'd talked about the day when he might play for Northwestern. Now he was chucking everything for what? A stupid ballet? Monty tried to stay cool.

"That's what you say today—"

"And that's what I'll say tomorrow. And the next day. Dad, I love the ballet." As Theo stood, Monty realized that even in his stocking feet, his son was a tad taller.

"Well, maybe this year. Just this year." Monty felt his face grow warm. "There's no future in dance, you know."

"Maybe yes, maybe no." Theo was in perfect control,

while Monty felt unhinged.

"You wanta be one of the guys, Theo. Believe me, being one of the guys is important."

"Maybe yes, maybe no," his son repeated. "I hope you and Mom'll be proud."

"And I hope you're not sorry!" Monty turned to hide his disappointment and strode from the room before words he knew he'd regret could tumble from his mouth.

Helen

"Where the hell are you going?"

Peering over the top of yesterday's *Wall Street Journal*, Helen was startled to see Haley in the kitchen doorway with her suitcase.

"Taking off. I've had enough around here." Haley dropped her purse on the kitchen table beside Helen's coffee.

Helen recoiled. Everyone knew purses were filthy. Why would her sister put hers on the spot where they ate, for Lord's sake? She slid her mug and English muffin several inches from Haley's bag.

"But—" she protested.

"No buts," Haley twanged. "There's nothing for me here. A guy I met at Rigoni's is driving to O'Hare this morning. He offered to take me, so I found a flight that's going to Denver late this afternoon." She poured a cup of coffee but didn't bother to sit down. "Gonna check out the real estate market in Colorado."

Helen's mind swirled. The house. All its contents. Their dad. His future plans. The work piling up in her own office in New York.

"Damn it, Haley." She tried to control her voice. "How can you go off and leave me with all this?" Staring at the nubby place mat their mother had woven years ago, she couldn't bring herself to look at her sister.

"Oh you—you'll figure it out. You always do." Haley coughed, a ragged sound that revealed her years of smoking. "But me—I've gotta cash in on my opportunities when they come along."

Like four failed marriages and who-knew-how-many unreliable jobs, Helen thought.

"I'm going to the Springs to sell houses for a developer. The Colorado market's warming up and should be red hot for a few years." Haley poked the depths of her purse for her lipstick.

"But all this—" Helen couldn't imagine shouldering the entire load by herself. Besides, she was every bit as anxious as her sister to get the hell out of Rockwell.

"Like I said, sell the stuff and get what you can for the house. Oh—and send me a check for my half." Haley tried to cover the awkward pause that followed with a forced giggle.

"But Dad— What are we—" Helen knew their father, confused as he was, couldn't begin to comprehend the life-changing decisions that faced his daughters.

"Give him a kiss for me." Haley leaned over and extended a stiff hug to Helen. "He won't care. You've always been his girl anyway."

"But—"

"Oopsy! There's my ride now. Gotta go."

Helen watched numbly as her twin collected her purse and suitcase, her high heels clicking on the hardwood floor.

"Keep me posted!" were Haley's final words as she pulled the heavy door shut behind her.

Helen spent the day wandering through the house, poking through drawers, leaving them half open. She devoted an entire morning to the attic. Surveying the collection of toys and school papers from her father's childhood, she wondered if her grandmother had ever thrown away a single thing.

The basement was even worse, filled with cupboards stuffed with cracked china and bundles of musty clothes that had not been delivered to their designated rummage sales. At last she allowed herself a good cry on the worn bottom step of the warped basement stairs, then blew her nose and called her office in New York. She told rather than asked them that she'd need more time at home and would proof articles online for the next week.

After two more days, she couldn't believe how void of life the house felt. She missed the persistent requests for attention from her calico cat, Miss Adelaide, and was shaken by the depth of her loneliness when she realized she would have welcomed Haley's metallic voice. Seeking relief from the smothering solitude, she gathered her keys and wallet and headed for the garage.

As she steered "Black Beauty" through the streets of Rockwell, she recalled how much she'd hated this town and all its phoniness when she was growing up. Her mother had lived for parties at "the club" but actually didn't like most of the people there. The girls at school could only talk about cute boys from nearby towns and the latest fashions in *Seventeen*. Everyone had adored her baton-twirling sister and predicted Haley might even be Purdue's next Golden

Girl if she chose to go there. In spite of her bulky size, Helen felt invisible. No one cared about her interests. In fact, no one but her dad cared about her at all.

Eventually, "Black Beauty" found its way to the back lot of The Boulder. She checked her watch—just past noon— and parked the car. She'd never dreamed the place would be so busy and almost left when she realized she had to take one of the two remaining spots at the counter.

Slinging her purse over the back of the stool, she caught a glimpse of the guy next to her—that Simpkins kid who'd come in a few days ago looking like death munching on a cracker. She ordered black coffee, an egg-white omelet with whole wheat toast, and a side of warm applesauce, then began to size him up.

A man dedicated to his habits, she decided. He nibbled at the crust of his ham salad sandwich, then washed it down with a gulp of cream soda straight from the bottle. His dark green pants and light blue shirt were clean and pressed, but his shaggy red hair screamed for a stylist to trim it and tame the cowlick that stood straight up at the crown.

"Visiting here?" he asked at last.

Embarrassed that she'd been caught studying him, she focused her attention on her omelet.

"Not for long. I came to help my dad adjust to the nurs- ing home."

"Now I got you placed. Walt Hamilton's daughter, right?" When he turned and offered her his hand, his smile revealed a large space between his front teeth. A homely face but an honest one, she concluded. She returned his firm handshake but was saddened by the somber expression in his brown eyes.

"And you are—" she queried.

"Simpkins. Yep, one of Henry and Fayetta's kids. Youngest one, in fact."

"Right. You had two sisters in the class ahead of me. Twins?"

"Irish twins. Eleven months apart." He chuckled as he continued his pattern—two small bites from his sandwich, one swig of cream soda. "June Carter Simpkins and Loretta Lynn Simpkins."

"Named for the singers." Suddenly she was chagrined that she'd allowed her comment on the obvious to roll out.

"Yep. All of us nine kids were. Mom and Dad—well, they liked country music. Obviously.

"Me? I'm Floyd Cramer Simpkins. Officially. You know, for the great piano player. But everyone calls me Pudge."

She scanned his physique. "But you're not—"

"Nope. Not fat at all." He wiped his mouth and grinned again. "Guess when I was a baby I was round as a basketball. But once I started walking, I ran off all that lard. Been Pudge ever since."

As they eased into comfortable conversation, she was grateful for his company. She did remember that whole string of Simpkins kids that had been crammed into a small house on the Sweet Briar side of town. Pudge said he didn't recall her.

"But everyone in town knew your sister." He paused. "Real cute she was. My sister, Brenda Lee, wanted to be just like her—you know, popular with the boys."

They pondered this comment silently before she spoke.

"I need to get home." She reached for her purse. "That

damn sister of mine, popular as she was, took off for Colorado and left me with a ton of work."

"Like what?" He plucked a toothpick from a container by the napkins.

"Like generations of junk." She shook her head at the thought of the attic and basement. "Nobody in our family ever threw anything away."

He was quiet for a moment. "I might—well, I prob'ly could help you some," he offered hesitantly. "Miss D—you know, the one that owns this place—well, she's got me doing some stuff at her house. I kinda think she's making up jobs to keep me busy."

"Midwest?" She felt she might as well address the elephant in the room.

"Yep." He sipped his soda. "Damn bastards," he whispered. "Been there since I was a kid sweeping up after shifts. Worked myself up to line foreman before they pulled the rug out from under me last week."

She'd heard all sorts of rumors about how hard Midwest's closing was going to hit the people of Rockwell, but she hadn't given them another thought. Now she was face to face with one of the victims.

"Pudge—" She hesitated as an idea began to take shape. "Is it okay if I call you that?"

He fixed his solemn brown eyes on her and nodded.

"I really could use your help." She felt a surge of relief as she wondered if this homely, red-haired guy might bring some common sense into her houseful of clutter.

He shifted his toothpick. "How about I stop by your place after work this afternoon and see what you got?"

"Sure." She felt a ripple of hope.

"See you then." Scooping up his bill, he gave her one more gap-toothed grin before he headed for the cash register.

Pudge

A s he parked his pickup in front of the white two-story house everyone in town knew belonged to Walt Hamilton, he recalled the countless times his mom had asked him to drive her past it. She'd tell him to slow down, sigh, and complain about the fact that she'd never live in a place like that. Then she'd remind herself that her nine kids more than made up for a rich man's castle.

He wondered if Mom had been down this street lately. The whole property looked the way he felt—like a bank repo. Its peeling paint, grass nearly knee high, and oak branches of all sizes scattered over the yard told the world that the place had seen better days. He picked up a few of the larger limbs and tossed them into the back of the truck. On his way to the front door, he paused to study the withered remains of Mr. Hamilton's prized tulip beds, and made a mental note to ask Helen if she'd like to have them cleaned up.

He had no idea what to expect from the inside of the house, but he knew the moment he stepped inside the spacious hall that his mom would've been knocked right out of her white socks. As Helen took him through the living room, he realized there was nowhere to sit. Every available seat was stacked with newspapers and magazines. Even the top of the grand piano was covered with old music and dusty bric-a-brac.

Still, he could tell that at some point people had loved this home. The pattern of the heavy floral draperies matched the wallpaper and from what he could see, the upholstery on the chairs. The den, which Helen admitted was the room where she hung out, was cozy but cluttered. Imagine, he marveled, having a special room for watching TV.

Everything in the entire place was spilling over with stuff—unused bowls and plates piled on the kitchen counters, closets in all four upstairs bedrooms crammed with clothes that looked like costumes for a play, ancient towels that probably hadn't moved from their bathroom shelves in years. He swallowed hard as he recalled the iron-clad rule that his mom had enforced: "Always pick up after yourself." Why, their tiny two-bedroom shack on the far side of the Sweet Briar section had been neater than Walt Hamilton's showplace!

"As you can see," Helen confessed, "I've got my work cut out for me. We'll look at the attic and the basement, then we can talk about what needs to be done."

"Sure."

"My mother never could bring herself to get rid of anything," she explained as they climbed the uneven stairs to the attic. "After she died seven years ago, Dad didn't have the heart or the energy to tackle it all."

When a tour of the rest of the house revealed more of the same, Pudge wasn't sure he was up for the job either.

"Coffee? I made a fresh pot." Helen seemed eager to talk about what she'd need from him.

He hesitated before answering. He'd always liked the rich smell of coffee but never its taste. Cream soda was his drink.

"Sure."

She smiled and shoved aside a bunch of junk mail that littered the kitchen table.

"Milk and sugar?" she asked.

"Sure." He knew he'd have to doctor up the coffee in order to get it down. Dumping a generous spoonful of sugar and a small amount of milk into his cup, he tasted the bitter brew, then added more milk and sugar. Goll-dern, he thought, how do all those folks up at The Boulder drink this every day?

"I hope to go back to New York in a week," Helen said. "But you can see it's going to take more than a few days to get the house ready to sell."

"Yep," he agreed.

"If I can get the—" she paused and waved her hand around the pile on the table—"well, all of this—organized into a pile in each room or tagged somehow, I'd like for you to haul it away. Then we'll have to see about giving the house a good cleaning before I list it."

"Sounds like a plan. When'll you be back?"

"Late winter, I hope. I'll be swamped at work during the next few months."

"Is that a fact?" He had no idea what her job with a magazine involved or how it could be so demanding. He tasted his coffee and tried not to make a face. The stuff was even worse as it cooled down.

"Warmup?" she asked.

"I'm good." He wanted to bring up the topic of pay. Instead, he forced down another sip but had to put the mug back on the table. He stared at the murky brew.

"We need to agree on how much I'll pay you."

Jiminy, could she read his mind? He was glad she brought that up.

They discussed his other commitments. He reminded her that right now he still spent days at Midwest and worked a few evenings for Miss D, but he'd be free—way freer than he'd like—in February.

She considered his time line, then admitted there was no huge hurry. They decided she'd pay him by the hour and he should stop in before she left for New York to see what she wanted him to do.

As they stood in the front hall, she thanked him for coming.

"I noticed you were drinking cream soda at The Boulder." Her hazel eyes twinkled. "I'll make sure I have a good supply of that while you're here."

Dern, he thought, embarrassed that she noticed. His face grew warm as he changed the subject. "I'm wondering if it'd be okay if I cleaned up your dad's tulip beds. I bet those bulbs need to be dug up. I could thin 'em out and replant 'em so they'll bloom in the spring."

"Oh, that would be—well, just perfect!" When she glanced away. Pudge realized she didn't want him to see she'd teared up.

As he strolled down the long sidewalk to his truck, he

whistled "You've Got A Friend in Me" and picked up a few more limbs. For a rich city gal, he decided, Helen Hamilton was not half bad.

Helen

She felt a huge weight lift off her shoulders as she watched Pudge toss a handful of broken branches into the back of his truck. For the first time in her life, she'd completed a comfortable conversation in Rockwell with someone near her own age. Kids in school could never get over the fact that she was a twin to the cute-and-popular Haley, and her parents' country-club friends often murmured concerns among themselves that she was an ugly duckling. She knew what they were saying by the way they glanced her way and lowered their voices. Lord, she'd thought, she couldn't get out of Rockwell fast enough.

When the phone rang, she welcomed the clipped New England accent that could only belong to her boss, Malcolm Overmyer.

"What's new?" Before she could answer, he fired off the word that the fiftieth anniversary issue of *The Arch* was on the drawing board. "Need you back here as soon as possible."

"I'm hoping ten days max—"

"Not good enough. We've got copy from celebrity writers out the wazoo." He paused for a breath. "You know those people always need extra editing and hate being corrected."

The call-waiting beep interrupted his voice. She recognized the number as Haley's and decided not to cut off her boss.

"I'll try to wrap things up—"

"Do your best. We need you here."

Click. Conversation over—as was her time in Rockwell. She'd try to change her flight after she spoke with her sister. Dialing Haley's number, she let the phone ring three times.

"You caught me doing my nails." The voice was edgy, combative. "They were a mess."

"I bet." She allowed herself the luxury of a dry response. "What's the word?"

"That's what I wanted to ask you." Haley's shrill giggle pierced Helen's ears from the land-line receiver. "I hope you got a bunch of good nibbles on the house by now."

"By now? Haley, it's only been a couple of days! This is going to take—"

"Just sayin'. I need the money for a real estate deal I may be able to swing out here. I thought I could light a fire under ya, Sis."

Helen clamped her lips to keep from blowing her stack. Haley only called her "Sis" when she wanted something.

"You're going to have to cool your heels, Haley. You more than anyone else ought to know how much time it can take to sell a house—"

"And you—" Haley's voice was rising when the call-waiting signal broke into her tirade.

"Gotta go. I'll get back to you." Relieved, Helen pressed the button.

48

"Hey, Babe." The gravelly tones of Burton Meyer had the same soothing effect as a cup of her favorite tea and a tranquilizer. For the last twelve years she'd felt herself relax when she spoke with her significant other. He always reminded her she'd rescued him from the garbage dump of humanity after his wife left with their two kids. He'd given her credit for helping him energize his struggling career as an entertainment attorney after they'd met at a dismal party in a West Village apartment. They always agreed they didn't want to ruin their relationship with marriage; things were too good the way they were.

Burt allowed her to unload the pressures of her previous conversations as she wailed about the impatience of her sister and the necessity of trying to be in two places at once.

"Cool it," he advised her, reminding her that where Haley was concerned, she was letting the tail wag the dog. "You make the decisions. Don't let her bully you. And as for Malcolm, he'll be glad to get you back whenever you can make it. Miss Adelaide and I are doing fine. I check on her every day."

She felt tears well up in her eyes. Lord, she was lucky to have Burt in her life!

"And one more thing," he added. "I miss you—and I'm not as patient as Malcolm."

Thank God for Burt, she thought as she hung up. And thank God for Pudge. She'd call him again that evening.

Pudge

The prospect of a temporary job lifted his spirits for the rest of the day, especially when Kristi heaved a huge sigh of relief and told him at supper that she thought it was great he could help Helen Hamilton.

"It's always good to do something for someone else." She brushed her auburn hair from her face and covered his hand with hers.

That was one thing about his wife that had drawn him to her when they first met at Rockwell High. Always positive, she had a kind word for everyone. But the night he'd told her about losing his job at Midwest, she shed angry tears as they tried to watch "Wheel of Fortune."

"Damn!" She'd choked back tears. "You've given them the best years of your life—and look how they paid you back."

He tried to paint a rosy picture, assuring her that they'd get along for awhile on her salary from the school. And he'd find something else. He knew he would.

A few days later he decided to order a grilled cheese for lunch at The Boulder. Maybe a change of menu would lift his spirits. He looked up as he heard Miss D's cane heading his way.

"Almost done fixing up your bathroom," he told her.

Miss D nodded and took the stool next to him.

"No ham salad?" She raised her eyebrows. "That's not like you."

"Just trying something different." He savored the sweetness of the cream soda as it slid down his throat, marveling at the fact that some folks around here knew you better than your own family. Miss D sure was one of them.

"Bathroom's lookin' good. Mallory's real happy with the change."

"Yep." He knew Miss D was trying to keep the house the way she liked it but make it nice for her granddaughter's family, who had lived there since the boating accident. "Wallpaper's out. Paint's in. Gotta keep up with the times."

"Sure glad to see you, Pudge."

"Always glad to see you, too, Miss D." No matter what was going on in his life, he always liked their chats.

"I've got a proposition for you."

"More work?" He knew Kristi was beginning to resent the time he spent doing odd jobs for Miss D, but they sure could use the money.

"No, no, no. This isn't about work." She signaled for Tiffany to bring her a cup of coffee. "This is about something you could do next month."

He wished she'd tell him what she had on her mind. Her kids were good about taking her to out-of-town doctor appointments, so she must not need help for that. At last she turned and fixed her gray eyes on him.

"Your mom's always liked country music, right?"

"You bet." He chuckled. "Why do you think she named all of us kids for country singers? Well," he added. "Everyone but me. Floyd Cramer was—"

"A damn good piano player," she finished. "My brother Tommy loved his music. You oughtta be proud to have that name."

"I am." As he polished off his grilled cheese, he wondered where Miss D was going with this. At last she came to the point.

"How'd you like to take your mom to the Grand Ole Opry?"

He almost slid off his stool as he tried to picture that. His mom at the place she'd always wanted to go more than anywhere in the world. "She'd think she won the lottery. Not gonna happen though."

"But it could, Pudge. It really could." Her words poured out faster than water from a downspout. Her son, David, had called from his home in Atlanta the day before. He and his wife had rented a little house in Nashville for three nights in October with tickets to the Opry, like they'd done every fall for the last few years. The whole package was non-refundable, but David had learned he had to stay home for an important company board meeting. Everything—the place to stay and the tickets too—were Pudge's. If he wanted them.

"Wait a minute. You're shi—uh, kidding me, right?"

"I'm not shittin' you, Pudge. This is for real."

"But—I'll still be at Midwest—"

"The hell with Midwest. What're they gonna do? Fire you? You've got vacation time."

"Uh—"

"Don't spend any time thinkin' about it. Just do it," she urged. "Third week of October oughtta be real nice down there. Besides, how many chances will you ever have to take your mom to Nashville?"

"I—I'll have to ask Mom—"

"Hell, Pudge, don't ask her. Tell her!" She gave him a confident smile.

"I'll run over to her house tomorrow. Right after work." He picked up a toothpick and headed for the cash register. "If Mom can go, she's gonna think she's died and gone to heaven."

Pudge

October

He'd been afraid his mother would come up with all sorts of reasons why she needed to stay home, but she jumped on the idea like a kid at Christmas. When his boss at Midwest said they needed him at work, Pudge shrugged and explained he was dipping into the vacation time he'd accumulated.

He was surprised that Helen seemed so excited about his trip. She was full of advice as they walked through her house and mapped out a plan for him to use when he started her project the first of February.

"Be sure to take water and snacks for the car," she reminded him.

"And some of Mom's favorite country music tapes," he added.

When Helen raised her eyebrows, he said his truck was so old it still had a tape player. She'd looked around her crowded living room and agreed it was okay after all to hang on to a few things from the past.

The morning of their departure, he made a bet with himself that his mom would be ready when he got to her place. Sure enough, she was waiting in the living room of the one-bedroom house his brother, Clyde, bought for her about seven years ago. "Red," as his brother was known in the Key West entertainment world, often sent her a little spending money when he'd had an extra-good gig.

After having seen the Hamilton place, he admired his mom more than ever for the way she kept house. Maybe, he thought as he picked up the suitcase she borrowed from one of his sisters, she could give Helen lessons on tidiness.

"Patsy thought I oughtta take her cooler too. You can carry that, and I'll bring my purse and crochet bag." Her words came in puffs, showing how excited she was. He'd never seen his mom looking so cute. She wore the new turquoise slacks and one of the crazy print tops that his oldest sister, Kitty, bought for her at Walmart in Danville. Sister Goldie had given her a perm that made her white hair coil real close to her pink scalp.

He locked the door behind them and steered her down the sidewalk.

"Don't be thinkin' you gotta take care of me ever minute," she chided. Then she flashed her scraggly grin to let him know she was teasing. A few years ago after she lost two bottom teeth, brother Red offered to pay for dentures, but she told him in no uncertain terms she wasn't "gonna be wearin' no fake teeth."

Pudge smiled and helped her into the truck. They'd had fun planning their trip, but when he mentioned he might get a GPS from one of his sibs, his mom told him not to.

"Ever time I ride with Patsy she's got the woman that talks on that thing buttin' in and tellin' us whur to turn."

She chattered a mile a minute as they drove to Danville and picked up I-74 to head toward Indy. But by the time they were on I-65 pointed south toward Nashville, her head lolled to one side and she dozed off. Deciding against waking her to see the red and gold trees that lined the highway, he turned down the music and allowed himself to think his own thoughts.

He'd never been much of a traveler. But once in awhile, Midwest had sent him into the south side of Chicago to pick up parts so he felt at ease on the interstate. He and Kristi never had extra money for trips, but they had a lot of fun camping with the kids several times at the state park about twenty miles from home. Brother Roy brought his camper from his place near Bakers Corners for them to use.

Moving into the slow lane as a semi threatened to gobble him up, he recalled those times at the campground. The four of them fished before breakfast and after supper. They swam in the lake and hiked the trails the rest of the time. The best part was their campfires, when Pudge told them old stories his mom dredged up from her childhood in Kentucky—stuff about ghosts that lived in deserted houses and monsters that attacked and ate people while they were in their own beds. Didn't bother his family a bit, he thought with a smile. They all slept like babies.

In southern Indiana he guided his pickup down an exit ramp and pulled into a truck stop that advertised McDonald's and Subway. Although his mom didn't think she needed to go inside, he insisted they visit the restrooms and have a bite of lunch. He thought he'd never get her out of the gift shop.

"Don't buy anything here," he cautioned. "You'll have plenty of time in Nashville."

She hummed to herself as she fastened her seat belt, then marveled at the way the hills had been carved right down the middle to make way for the road.

"Looks like they took a chunk out of a great big three-layer cake," she observed.

He thought he'd have to tie her down when they crossed the Ohio River. She hadn't seen that much water in one place since she and her family moved from Kentucky when she was a girl. As they wound their way through Louisville, she couldn't believe "somebody built all them tall buildings so close together." On the way out of the city she squealed in terror when a jet roared over their car as it prepared to land at the airport.

She commented that all the Mammoth Cave billboards and rusty-roofed tobacco barns tucked into the hillside reminded her of scenes from her childhood in Kentucky. He took a fast look at the Corvette Museum in Bowling Green and made a mental note to come back with his brother Roy.

"Sure wish I had a dollar for ever one of them orange barrels," she observed as he wove the truck through construction zones near Nashville.

"You'd be one rich lady."

Referring to the map he'd memorized, he took them past rows of look-alike hotels, made a few turns, and pulled up in front of a small house.

"Would you get a load of all them pansies." His mom took a deep breath. "S'pose they knowed I love purple?"

Inside, she explored the cottage from end to end, commenting that she might have picked out "purtier" furniture for the place but delighting in the kitchen and its sparkling appliances.

"Why, I could cook us supper right here if I had to." She nodded as she mentally took possession of her new surroundings. Realizing that was the supreme compliment, Pudge whistled as he carried in their suitcases.

During their three-day stay in Nashville, he had more fun watching his mom's reactions to "all them people in one place" than exploring the city itself. Each morning she gabbed so freely with a couple of the waitresses at the Waffle House that he wondered if they might end up on his mom's Christmas card list. After they boarded the tour bus, she was glued to the window, soaking up all the sights Nashville had to offer. But nothing compared to the Opryland Hotel, where she stared with her fork in the air as they ate lunch.

On Saturday night when he coaxed his truck into a narrow spot in the Grand Ole Opry House parking lot, his mom said she oughtta pinch herself to make sure she was still alive. Inside the famed auditorium, she fell into a reverent silence. As the country stars began to perform, however, she erupted with louder cheers than most teens could muster.

"Wahoo!" she called as soon as Lee Ann Womack finished her song. Then she leaned closer to Pudge and whispered, "Her skirt's way too short!"

Eventually, he realized that some portions of the show were done for radio and others for TV. After four-and-a-half hours he suggested they might want to leave "to beat the traffic." His mom agreed but said she wanted to buy some souvenirs before they went home. When they left the auditorium she turned to take in one last look at the place that had been the source of her Saturday night entertainment most of her life.

Pudge felt almost dizzy as they wandered through the endless rows of Opry keepsakes. After much deliberation, she decided to splurge on a framed composite picture of the old Ryman Auditorium overlaid with the current Grand Ole Opry Hall to put up in her kitchen. She picked out a fancy mug for Pudge and key chains for "ever one of my kids," explaining that she'd wait and send Brenda Lee's at Christmas.

The next morning before they left she hugged the girls at the Waffle House while he grabbed a toothpick and paid the bill.

"On to Kentucky," he announced. "Last leg of the trip. Are you sure you still want to find the spot where you lived till you were seven?"

She ran her tongue through a gap where a bottom front tooth should have been—a sure sign she was stressed.

"I cain't tell you what a hankerin' I have to see if it matches the picture I have in my head."

"But—" he tried to protest as they merged onto the interstate.

"I know, I know. We heard a few years ago that a couple from Ohio bought our old house and tore it down. I guess they put up a real nice place. I—" She paused for a moment. "I just wanta see, Pudgey, if it <u>feels</u> the same. After that, I can die happy."

"You shush, you hear?" he scolded.

Snugging her purse close to her chest, she gazed at the hills, deep in her own thoughts. At last they left the interstate and began winding their way down a two-lane road. When he turned past a ramshackle building onto a road called Mulberry Hollow, she sat up straight.

"Wrong way, Pudgey! Wrong way! You gotta go a little bit farther down that main road."

"But Mom—"

"No siree bob," she insisted. "Didja see the slant on the roof of that old building? That there's the old Stuckey's, and we always turned at the road after it. Not at that corner."

He obliged, made a U-turn, and crunched through the gravel back to the two-lane highway.

"This road ain't much now, but back when I was a kid it was real busy. Afore the interstates." She sat as tall as she could.

"Looks like there's more rust than roof on the old Stuckey's," she muttered. "Now, go that-a-way and turn right at the next road."

Swallowing his protest, he did as he was told. He sure didn't want to go against her wishes, but he didn't feel the need to get lost in the hills of Kentucky.

"Okay. Now slow down. Right here."

A crooked wooden sign told him they were in Fergus Gulch. Probably not even on a GPS, he figured. He put the truck in second gear as they chugged up a steep hill overrun with wild bittersweet. Hesitating at a fork in the road, he waited as his mom studied both lanes and jabbed her finger left.

"That 'un there. It's comin' back to me now."

He felt his palms grow clammy as the lane narrowed. If

she was wrong, there was nowhere to turn around. Goll-dern, he wished he'd stuck with their original plan to go straight home from Nashville.

"Round the bend, Pudgey," she encouraged him. But when they turned the corner, there were only brambles crowding the road. "Little farther than I remembered," she whispered.

"Mom—I've gotta turn around somehow. This road's taking us nowhere, and it's petering out."

"Keep her goin.'"

He sure hated to disappoint her, but they were on a snipe hunt—no doubt about it. He'd watch for the first good place where there was enough space to ease the truck around so they could get out of this godforsaken place.

One more turn—not enough room. Another . . . and now the lane was hardly wide enough for his truck. He'd check the next bend, then throw the truck into reverse and start backing up.

"There it is." He barely heard his mom's soft words of wonder.

"There it is!" This time she shouted like a kid and pounded the dashboard with her fist.

Ahead lay a well maintained log cabin with a front porch, sturdy green metal roof and—much to his relief—a driveway where he could make a turn.

"Park right here for a minute. I gotta get out. Looks like nobody's home."

Leaving her purse on the front seat, she slid down from the truck. He joined her, straining to listen as they strolled around the yard.

"New folks musta put in indoor plumbing." She took a few more steps. "Back there's where our outhouse stood. And my daddy's woodshed.

"It's all so differ'nt now. But that tree—the big oak behind them redbuds and dogwoods?" He followed her into the side yard. "That's where—oh, my god—would you look at that?"

He stopped and stared. From a sturdy limb hung a new piece of rope attached around a tire to make a swing.

"They've went and tied a rope to a tire. Just like we done. All those years ago."

He glanced away when he saw tears rolling down her cheeks.

"Me—me 'n my sister—we'd swing for hours on the tire that Daddy brung home from town one night. We thought if we went high enough, we could crack open the floor of heaven."

He wanted to capture this moment forever—the picture he had in his mind of a skinny pigtailed girl giggling as she flew as high as the old tire would take her.

He let her linger until she told him they'd better get back to the main road and head for home. After he inched the truck around in the driveway and started their descent, he heard his mom say something about this "bein' ever bit as good as the Opry."

Although their side trip had added hours to their journey, he was grateful they'd taken the time. When his mom admitted she was worried about having to travel after dark, he suggested they have a leisurely supper and spend the night at a motel. They found a decent truck stop and checked in at a place next door, where the aging owner welcomed them warmly. His mom didn't think much of the bars of soap "the size of a pat of butter" but slept soundly in her double bed.

The following day on the way home she filled his head with stories—more family lore than he'd ever heard. She told him how her daddy had to leave the coal mines and find work up north. Then she recalled how she met her future husband in fourth grade at Sweet Briar School.

"Henry Simpkins—such a sweet boy. So poor. Always had bruises on his face and arms, but he smiled at me ever day." She fell quiet again before she continued.

"After all the lickin's your pa took from his old man, he vowed he'd never whup any of you with a belt." She shook her head. "And he never did."

She spoke of how she and his pa tried to train "all nine of you kids" to be honest and work hard. "Some of you listened better'n others," she added, "but we was blessed."

When she paused again, he knew she was remembering Brenda Lee, who only sent a card at Christmas, and Ernie, who'd done time in Alabama when a get-rich-quick scheme backfired.

"We never had a car till you was in high school, Pudgey. But remember how the whole bunch of us'd walk uptown on Saturday night and get four nickel cones to share? Then we'd watch all them people who had enough money to buy hamburgers and fries come out of the cafe and go to the show."

"Those were good times," he assured her.

"And then we'd walk back home, and I'd make popcorn and we'd listen to the Opry."

The thought of the Opry and the fact she'd been there

silenced her again.

"Funniest thing," she said as they crossed the state line into Illinois, "I never knew them country stars was singin' to so many people in such a big place. When we heard 'em at home, it seemed like they was singin' just to us."

"It did, Mom. It did."

As he pointed the truck up the road toward home, he stole a glance at his mother. Of all of us kids, he thought, nobody ever had her to themselves the way I did on this trip. And, although he was itching to see Kristi after having been gone for four nights, he knew right then he'd never have a moment as satisfying as this one if he lived to be a hundred.

Doris

"Have you seen Pudge the last coupla days?" Doris continued to strip meat from the chickens she'd simmered all morning. "I'll swear. He hasn't smiled like that since before he got screwed over by Midwest." She paused. "Sorry, honey. I do try to use better language when I'm with you, but sometimes I forget."

Cherisse grinned. "That's okay, Grando. I've heard way worse'n that on the playground since I was in second grade."

Doris paused as she picked out scraps around a neck bone. Another good thing about Sweet Briar, she thought to herself. Kids really learn their cuss words at an early age.

"Scoot that thing over here." Doris nodded toward a faded yellow mixing bowl on the restaurant's kitchen counter. "I'll show you how to strip the meat off the chicken so you'll know how to do it right." She pretended not to notice the shadow of reluctance that passed over Cherisse's face.

"Wouldn't it be easier to buy this already cut up?" Her great-granddaughter made a face as she pulled a chunk of white meat from a bone. "This must be the worst job in all of cooking."

"And you're starting with a nice thick piece." Doris grinned and snatched up the breasts, then dropped two bony backs onto Cherisse's cutting board.

"First thing—and listen real hard—you don't get the flavor when you buy that canned stuff. Clean hands, maybe, but no taste." She glanced at her own slimy fingers. "You gotta do this when the chicken's still warm, then you gotta dig deep down into the tiny spots around the bones. That's where you'll get your flavor. Here. See what you can do with these."

She watched as Cherisse gingerly poked into the cavities and came up with a few strands of tender meat. Satisfied, Doris returned to her original topic.

"Pudge said Fayetta and him even went out of their way so she could see the spot where she lived as a little girl in Kentucky."

"Hmm." Cherisse wrinkled her nose as she studied her greasy hands.

"I always liked the way Fayetta and Henry raised their kids. Made hard workers out of all of 'em. Well, maybe not Ernie. He always tried to take too many short cuts." She started to disassemble a wing, then thought better of it and tossed it onto Cherisse's board.

"I used to feel sorry for Fayetta back when we were in school. She was too poor to fit in and she knew it. It's no wonder Henry Simpkins took a shine to her. He was worse off 'n she was." She stopped to check out Cherisse's work and was pleased to see that the backbones hadn't a morsel left on them.

"If it hadn't been for the Fearless Four, I'd have been up

shit creek myself. Oops. Sorry, honey." She scolded herself for letting her old language slip out. "Don't you grow up talkin' like your Grando."

"What d'ya mean about not fitting in?" Pulling the last piece from the cooker, Cherisse looked relieved when she realized she'd get to work on a plump thigh instead of a back.

"Well, I've told you about my friends. Rosie you've met. Cheryl, the singer, who's mainly blind now but calls me once in awhile. And Kate—God rest her soul—who was tryin' to fit in too." She sighed as she remembered. "The things we did together. I wouldn't trade a minute with those girls for all the tea in China."

"I wish I had a Fearless Four. Kids at school have what they call friend groups, and you're either in or you're out. I have a couple of girls I do stuff with, but I sure don't have a friend group." Attacking the thigh, she tore every last shred of meat from the bone.

"How come?"

"I'm not like them, Grando." Cherisse sorted through the stack of bones, pulling out a few pieces that still contained bits of meat. "They think I'm weird 'cause I'm a big NASCAR fan. But I don't care. I love the races!"

"Then you go to 'em with Dougie and Maria, you hear? Don't let some silly girls change you or you'll lose your flavor." She paused. "Like canned chicken."

"And there's one other thing," Cherisse sounded hesitant as she stared at the pile of meat she had just accumulated. "I like English. And nobody else does. They think I'm a freak."

"Well, how about that!" Doris felt joy and pride swell inside her. "People call you 'Little Doris' cause they say we're so much alike. Except you got black hair." She slapped the counter. "But here's where we're different—me'n you."

"My teacher says I'm good," Cherisse admitted.

"Well, then, you keep on bein' good. Here—you can take this trash outside for me. But before you do, I gotta tell you. I remember another girl who didn't fit in. She was good at English too, and now she's got some high-powered job in New York."

"Really?" Cherisse brightened up.

"You know her too. I'm talkin' about Helen Hamilton. Me'n her dad, Walt, was in high school together."

"That lady who's been in here lately? The one who dresses nice even when she's bumming?"

"That's the one." Doris smiled. "A twin, would you believe it? I seen both of 'em the other day, but I think the sister's left town already. A real piece of work, that one is."

"A twin? But not identical, right?" Cherisse seemed intrigued.

"You got it, honey. You never met two more different people in your life." She made a mental note to be sure her great-granddaughter got to meet Helen Hamilton. Cherisse might be floored if she realized what a success Helen had become—and all because she could write a decent sentence. In the meantime, Cherisse was showing signs that she might fit into a place of her own—right here in the kitchen at The Boulder.

PART II

2013

Pudge

February

He wished he had a bottle of that happy feeling he and his mom had shared so he could turn it loose after Christmas. Once the holidays were over, his life seemed to slide downhill on a slippery slope.

First, Kristi—the most optimistic person in his life—started circling ads in the "Help Wanted" column of the newspaper. He didn't want to work as an early-morning carrier for the Danville *Commercial-News*, and the idea of selling insurance for an out-of-town company tied his stomach in knots.

"Just some suggestions." His wife gave him a wan smile.

Then the kids started in on him.

"I think I might skip night classes this term," Jenna announced when she came in from her day shift as an aide at Happy Haven. "I heard there's a lady in Bakers Corners looking for someone to stay with her at night and the pay's not bad."

"No way! You keep working toward getting into nurse's

training and I'll find <u>something</u>," said Pudge.

He hadn't been able to bring himself to look up from the bag of recyclables he was tying up to haul to the curb. It would break his heart to see his daughter, her freckled face full of hope, postpone her own dream to help with family expenses. When Mason opened his mouth to speak, Pudge felt trapped.

"And don't you think about giving up your night classes either!" he snapped at his son. "I'm going over to Mom's to check on her before supper."

As the frigid air pierced his lungs, he felt his head begin to clear.

Shoot, he thought, he'd never been in such a pickle in his entire life. He had two days left at Midwest before they shut the place down, and he wasn't sure he could handle it. Since the day he'd picked up a broom and swept out the factory when he was a junior in high school, Midwest had been the center of his world. He'd come to think of it as a second home as he advanced through the ranks.

He liked to have things orderly in his life—no surprises. No sirree! Especially a big one like losing his job. He shivered as he realized his whole body felt like someone had put it in a vise and tightened the screws, like his skin was one size too small. Thank God he could go see his mom, he thought as he parked in front of her house.

"Pudgey!"

His mom greeted him from her chair like he was the person she loved most in all the world. He felt his body relax as he knelt and hugged her.

"Smells good in here, Mom." He pulled off his jacket

and tossed it on her davenport. "What're you making?"

"I cooked up a batch of stew—thought you and Kristi and the kids might like it." She held up the afghan she was crocheting. Splashes of purple, pink, and fuchsia cascaded down her lap.

"Thought I'd make somethin' special for Brenda Lee." Averting his eyes, she concentrated on her stitches. "When I get her address."

"But her Christmas card came back. You don't even know—"

"I'll get it some of these days. And 'en I'll send it to her." She counted her stitches. "To remind her she's still got family back here. Wherever she is."

He felt his gut turn over. That sister of his! How could she treat their mom like this—heading out west and never keeping in touch? He wanted to unload all his frustrations. Right here. Right now. Instead, he said, "She's gonna love it, Mom. I think it's the prettiest one you've ever done."

"And I've done a bundle." Her brow furrowed as she told him about his brother, Ernie, who'd called from Mississippi the night before and asked for a few bucks to tide him over.

"Hated to admit I don't have the money. Heat bill's gone up and there's them new pills—well, you know what I mean."

He knew too derned well what she meant. Ernie usually managed to keep one step ahead of the law because of the schemes he got tangled up in, but at least he still checked in with their mom. Pudge diverted their conversation from her two kids who were the most worrisome and confessed he was scared about the closing of Midwest.

They talked about bumps in the road of life, as she called them. He felt warm, reassured as she recounted a few of the rough times she and his pa had. And as she expressed her faith that "God'll take care. Always has and always will," he realized she hadn't spent all those Sundays at the Baptist Church for nothing.

"And Pudgey, sometimes He'll surprise you." She went to the kitchen and returned with two plastic sherbet tubs filled with stew. "Look how we got surprised with that trip to Nashville."

He leaned down so she could plant a kiss on his cheek.

"Most fun I ever had," she murmured.

"Me too, Mom. Thanks for supper." When he stepped outside the cold air jarred him, and he quickly closed the door. He didn't want his mother's expensive heat to escape.

On the way home he marveled at her calm ability to cope. In spite of losing his job, he realized he was one lucky dude. His family would gobble up his mom's stew tonight. And the next two days at Midwest? He'd have to cross those bridges one day at a time.

Monty

He loved his Beemer. He really did. Sometimes he thought of it as his mobile clone—durable, dependable, and ready for any challenge. There were moments, however, when his car appeared to have a mind of its own. This seemed to be one of those times as he felt the car turn into Rockwell and point toward The Boulder.

The whole day had started off in a crazy way. First, Claire and Theo were in a twitter over the scholarship his son had been offered to a ballet camp in Colorado. Since *The Nutcracker*, when Monty had felt more bewildered than proud at Theo's graceful performance, their lives had revolved around dance. Cassidy grumbled the previous night that if she wanted to get any attention, she guessed she'd better quit her basketball team and take up ballet.

Then she cranked up her phone and danced defiantly to "Call Me Maybe" when she left the room. She knew her dad was sick of the song and did it to bring his temper to the boiling point. He took a deep breath and glanced away; he didn't need an ugly scene with his daughter right now!

Next, Al's girlfriend had called first thing that morning

and said Al was down with stomach flu and wouldn't be going anywhere. Although Monty expressed his disappointment, he felt relieved he'd have the day to himself. He wasn't due in Danville until 2 p.m. and wouldn't need to rush.

When he opened the door to The Boulder, he was surprised to find plenty of empty booths. He took one near the front and ordered from the same ponytailed server who'd been there in September. As she scribbled his order he heard a voice calling in his direction.

"Wondered if you'd ever come back and see us." He cringed when he realized the elderly lady who'd chatted with Al and him was striding toward his booth as fast as her cane would allow. "Coffee's on me, remember? I'm Doris—Doris Lochschmidt. Okay if I sit for a few minutes?"

Before he could reply, she leaned on her cane and seated herself across from him.

"Where's your buddy?"

He could tell she was on a quest for information. "Down with stomach flu." He paused as she processed this morsel. "I'm on my way back to Danville by myself."

"Glad you came. Even gladder he didn't if he's sick. We got enough problems here as it is."

He admired the plateful of golden brown French toast dusted with confectioners sugar the server placed in front of him.

"Just coffee for me, Tiffany." Mrs. Lochschmidt gave his order a look of approval. "Glad to see you liked the French toast enough to come back for more."

"How did you remember?" He drizzled syrup over the slices. "That was a few months ago."

"It's something you pick up over the years. I've been at it awhile."

She'd come to talk but would be challenged to speak over the raucous chortle of a man in the booth behind him and the clatter of dishes as a teen-age boy cleared the center tables. Forking a large bite into his mouth, he relaxed. His mother would've loved this place. Claire not so much.

"How long have you been here?" He had a hunch she wanted him to ask.

"Since 1982. See, it says right here." She reached across the table and ran her finger along the typed message on his place mat. "Me 'n my sister Violet had started a catering business and decided to go whole hog with a restaurant. Violet's been gone for a few years now. Her mind left a long time before her body gave out. Terrible thing."

She paused to reflect on her sister's absence. "Now my daughter Darcy runs the place. That's her girl Tiffany who waited on you." She sipped her coffee. "Me? I bake a pie once in awhile and come in every day to make sure things're goin' good."

"Sure tastes like it. Where did you learn to cook like this?"

Resisting the urge to check his watch, he regretted he'd asked such a loaded question. He felt as if he'd opened the floodgates when all of Mrs. Lochschmidt's background poured out—how she left her husband and raised six kids, how the restaurant struggled and she and Violet almost lost it, and, finally, how it somehow emerged as Rockwell's gathering place.

"Always catered to the kids, the pride of our town," she

explained as he soaked up the remaining syrup with his last bite of toast. "If you've got a minute, I'd be pleased to show you our pictures on the wall up front."

He allowed his eyes to sweep over his watch and realized it wouldn't hurt him to take a quick look. Besides, she was already out of the booth and expecting him to follow.

He studied the grainy black-and-white pictures of basketball players from the late 1940s—her brothers Vic and Charley Panczyk, who'd taken Rockwell to the state finals. He listened as she repeated the litany of other great athletes who put their town on the map.

"Looks like basketball talent has run pretty deep around here." His sigh was so profound that Mrs. Lochschmidt glanced sharply at him.

"Yeah—and it's a good thing. Like this year. Maybe if we win the sectional, that'll help ease the pain of losin' Midwest. You like basketball?" she wondered as they headed back to their booth.

Checking his watch, he felt he could linger another five minutes and thanked Tiffany as she filled his cup. "I played a little. At Northwestern."

"I knew I liked you!" She beamed. "Your kids play?"

He squirmed as he told her his daughter was developing into a strong guard and felt a twinge in his gut when he mentioned his son had quit the high-school team earlier in the season.

"For dance, can you believe it?" He shook his head. "To be a damn ballet dancer!" The lump in his throat prevented him from saying more.

"Had a brother like that. My youngest one." She spoke

reverently. "Was rough on him, coming along on the heels of Vic and Charley the way he did. Everyone in town thought he'd be another star, but all he wanted to do was play the piano."

"Hard on everyone," he agreed.

"You know what though? Tommy was damn good. Did his own thing for a long time in New York."

"Tommy?" Slowly he tried to connect the name to the brothers whose pictures lined the walls. Their name had been—Panczyk. "Your name was Panczyk, right? Was your brother the Tommy Panczyk?"

"You heard of him?" Her eyes sparkled.

"Who hasn't? My god, wait'll I tell my wife!"

"Might wanta tell that boy of yours too." She winked. "You never know."

He picked up his bill, thanked her for joining him, and promised that he'd be back.

"Good thing," she replied. "Our crowd's kinda slim these days."

There were a lot of empty seats, he realized as he waited at the cash register for his credit card to clear. Mrs. Lochschmidt had stopped to chat with a red-haired guy who was sipping cream soda at the counter.

"Only one more day, then we're done there," Monty heard the fellow say. "But I've got all that work to do at the Hamilton house for now. We'll get along."

"You tell your mom hello for me." Mrs. Lochschmidt gave him a friendly pat on the back.

"Will do. I'm on my way there right after work," he assured her.

Poor rube, Monty thought, as he signed his receipt. Stuck in a small town with no job. He'd hate to be in that guy's shoes with no schedule and no career plan and not the vaguest idea of how to start one.

He turned the key in his Beemer, refreshed from his stop and reassured by the knowledge that his own life remained well-ordered and under control. He and Claire had hit a few snags with Theo, but Monty vowed he'd steer him away from ballet and back to basketball before long. One way or another.

His thoughts turned to Mrs. Lochschmidt's brother. He couldn't wait to tell Claire that Tommy Panczyk had grown up here. And that he'd chosen piano over basketball!

As he pulled onto the highway, he reconsidered. He wasn't sure he wanted to share that last part with his wife and certainly not with Theo.

Pudge

He felt like he was trudging through a black cloud as he and his fellow workers left Midwest at quitting time. No one uttered a word, but they shared a single thought: Only one more day. For a guaranteed job. And a guaranteed paycheck.

His pickup headed for his mom's almost as if it knew the drill. Although he stopped each afternoon to check on her, he'd realized lately that what he wanted was her reassurance, that he needed her words to soothe his nerves.

"Hey, Mom." He closed the door behind him. "It's me."

Conversation from her favorite soap blanketed the room. Seemed she'd been cranking up the volume an awful lot these days.

"Goll-dern," he whispered to himself. "She's gone to sleep in spite of all this racket."

She looked contented, so peaceful with her afghan in her lap. He sure hated to wake her. But still—

"Mom." He nudged her arm. She didn't respond. "Mom!" he shouted. She felt cold. Her feisty energy had left. Just gone. Someplace. But where? Frantically his eyes searched the room for evidence that his mother was still there.

"Mom!" Only sounds from the scripted TV soap answered his plea. He could hardly control his shaking hand as he picked up the receiver of her rotary phone and dialed 911.

Helen

"I don't even want to think about going to Rockwell tomorrow."

Helen held a sack containing their Chinese take-out with one hand and linked her other arm through Burt's to steady herself on the icy sidewalk.

She'd always been grateful that years ago she'd found the one-bedroom condo on Bank Street in the West Village, and that Burt seemed as comfortable in her apartment as he did in his own Midtown place.

"You'll feel better once you get there," he assured her. Snowflakes dotted the broad shoulders of his navy overcoat as they waited to cross the intersection of Bank and Waverly Place. "What do you hear from the guy with the oddball name?"

She shook her head, the arctic air catching in her throat, and wondered again why brainy Burt with the steel-trap mind often stumbled over people's names.

"You know, Pudge never texts or emails, but I did catch up with him on his cell a few days ago." Helen dodged a miniature poodle who stopped to do his job right in front of her. She hoped the dog's adoring owner would use the plastic bag attached to the leash. "He started some basic cleanup on Dad's house and then a terrible thing happened."

"He got lost in the attic?" he quipped.

She stopped and faced him. "His mom died. Was totally unexpected." She brushed the snow from her face.

"Oh, poor guy." Burt switched from glib to sympathetic. "He has a bunch of siblings, right?"

"Yes, but he's really torn up. I could hear it in his voice." She paused, recalling Pudge's brief and unemotional responses to her questions. She felt as if she were talking with a mechanical device. "I asked him if he wanted me to delay my trip, but he told me to go ahead and come. He's already ordered a trash bin for a lot of the stuff in the house."

"Really?" Burt slowed his pace and fell behind as she reached for her key and headed up the steps to her brownstone. "That sounds pretty serious."

"You can't even imagine." She handed him her sack while she opened the door. "I wish you could see it. Before and after." When Burt didn't respond, she realized once more he'd probably never leave New York to go to Rockwell. "Pudge said he'd be glad to have the work and we should be able to make some good headway."

As she entered the long narrow living room that was her own private haven, she turned on lights while Burt put their food on the kitchen counter and found two glasses and a bottle of wine. Miss Adelaide rubbed against their legs before returning to her favorite cushion on the sofa.

"Damn cat," she heard Burt scold affectionately. Helen felt the tensions of the day slip away as she hit the power button on the TV remote and the strains of Vivaldi washed over her. Sipping the wine Burt handed her, she allowed herself a moment to savor the ambiance of the room she had created. Her mother, during one of her rare visits, had called her furnishings "trash." Her friends kindly referred to them as "eclectic" or "zany." Helen rationalized the outlandish cost of the small Danish sofa by reminding herself that she paid nothing for the three cast-off wooden chairs she discovered on a neighborhood sidewalk and lugged home one at a time. After painting each a vibrant color, she asked a friend to stitch pads from material featuring illustrations from various children's books. She complimented herself when she found them more comfortable than anything in her dad's house. Her favorite books filled the floor-to-ceiling shelves on one wall, while various posters for old movies and Broadway shows occupied treasured space on her other walls. Her recently-purchased Scandinavian lamps dwelt on sleek tables and cast a soft but optimistic light over the entire room.

Using chopsticks, they ate in silence on stools at the counter. She knew Burt's mind was focused on a complicated court case that needed his full attention, and her own thoughts were on making her flight out of LaGuardia the next morning. She'd arranged for a car service to pick her up at Midway—expensive, she knew, but the best way to do it. Maybe, if she had longtime friends in Rockwell, she could've asked someone to meet her. And maybe, she hoped, the snow would accumulate and her flight would be canceled.

Burt interrupted her thoughts. "You're sexy when you're wearing that private smile. Especially when you have sweet-sour sauce on your cheek."

She dabbed her face with her napkin, then threw it at Burt in mock fury.

"You'll miss me when I'm gone," she reminded him.

"It won't be that long and it won't be that bad." He scraped the bottom of the chicken almond ding box with his spoon. "Only a week."

"It'll seem like a month," she lamented.

"Don't forget to hurry back." A mischievous grin spread across the wide face beneath his damp gray curls. "Remember—I have two tickets for *Picnic* in ten days. And I'd hate to have to ask someone else to go."

Pudge

It was all too much—too much food, too many people, too many decisions. Nothing was in its usual order the way he liked it. If it hadn't been for Kristi, he knew he couldn't have made it through the days after his mom's death.

His wife had a sixth sense about when to step up and when to step aside. She chatted with friends who brought casseroles and stayed too long, but she bowed out of his sisters' debate over the outfit Mom would be buried in. When his sibs had badmouthed Ernie for being too broke to fly home for the funeral, Kristi had encouraged each of them to thank their brother Red for putting that expense on his own credit card. And she'd sensed the exact times Pudge needed to be held. Quietly. He'd always be obliged to her for that.

He also knew he'd be forever grateful to Miss D for calling him the morning after he'd found his mom and telling him she'd talked with the ladies at the Baptist Church about having the funeral dinner at The Boulder. But they all agreed it would be best if Miss D and her crew brought the main dish to the church and let the ladies take care of salads and desserts.

"Fayetta and me went way back and I know she liked our meat loaf and chicken 'n noodles," Miss D reminded him. "Us Sweet Briar kids have always had a special bond, you know. I'd like to give her the best." Her voice had broken as she'd added, "She deserves it."

When they gathered in the church basement after the trip to the cemetery, his knees buckled at the sight of his family gathered to honor Mom. Well, all but Brenda Lee. Nobody'd been able to track her down.

Friends and relatives attacked the long tables loaded with food, then spilled onto the sidewalk to smoke and tell stories peppered with cuss words about how Fayetta had helped them in one way or another. His buddies from Midwest huddled around him like they felt he needed protection from the hullabaloo.

But there was no escaping. A crowd of friends and relatives followed him back to his house like they were stuck to him with duct tape. He wished he could be at Midwest taking care of his shift. At last, when no one was looking, he was able to ditch all of them and slip into his bedroom. Funny how it had worked out, he thought, as he unbuttoned his dress shirt and pulled on an old tee. He'd had his last day at the factory and never known it at the time. It had come and gone, and he hadn't even been there.

He allowed himself a few minutes to sit on his bed with his head in his hands as he realized his world had gone straight to hell. No job. No mom. No nothing to look forward to.

He was tempted to ignore his cell when it vibrated in his pocket. Instead, he picked it up. "Yeah?"

Helen Hamilton was on the line, expressing her sympathy and telling him he didn't need to come to her house this week. Yes, she'd flown in the day before and would start sorting business papers the next morning. The two of them could get organized in a few days when he felt like it.

Pudge stood and looked out the window at the dwindling mounds of gray snow, remnants from last week's storm. The next few days would be bedlam at his mom's as his brothers and sisters tried to decide what to do with all her stuff. He'd let them go at it. All he really wanted was her picture of the Ryman Auditorium and Grand Ole Opry Hall. And maybe the afghan she'd been working on. He'd keep it in case Brenda Lee showed up someday.

"Pudge? Are you in there?" A sharp knock signaled that his wife was looking for him.

"Sure. Just thinking." He nodded at Kristi as she opened the bedroom door.

"That's okay," he told Helen Hamilton. "I'll be there first thing tomorrow morning. About eight."

It would be good to have a reason to get out of bed the next day, he thought, as he braced himself for the crush of friends in his living room. He guessed he'd rather be dealing with someone else's old stuff than his mom's. That would've been way too much.

Helen

S he loved the way he treated her belongings with respect. Although Pudge worked quickly, he took an instant to evaluate each object before placing—never tossing—it into one of three piles: "Keep," "Sell," and "Salvation Army." They'd agreed the day before to separate the areas of the attic with yellow tape that Pudge bought at the Dollar Store.

By the middle of the second morning, she realized the whole place looked like a crime scene and she felt like a walking lint bunny. Pudge's hair flecked with grime that sifted down from the rafters had taken on a tweed effect. They'd dropped the niceties that filled their earlier conversations and spoke more like siblings.

"Here's a whole bunch of letters. Looks like they came from a soldier. Maybe World War I?" He paused to study the top envelope in a stack that filled a sagging Marshall Field's box.

"Oh, Lord. More family history shit." She groaned. "Better put those in with the 'Saves.' But I can't imagine when I'll ever have time to look at them."

She watched as he placed the bulging box on the seat of

a child's red rocker. Pudge looked so wan, she thought. His mom's death was taking its toll.

"Let's break for a few minutes. Ready for a soda?"

His gap-toothed grin lit up his peaked face. "Whatever you say, Miss H."

"That's another thing," Helen told him as they inched their way down the attic's dark narrow stairs and removed their sooty shoes. "Call me Helen. Please."

"But I always call Mrs. Lochschmidt 'Miss D,'" he protested. "Out of respect."

"That's what I mean." She fixed on him the tolerant look she sometimes gave new writers at *The Arch*. "Makes me feel like an old woman."

During their break she asked about his family and the shock they had experienced.

"Never been through anything like it." He studied his bottle before taking a drink. "Not even when Midwest dropped their bombshell."

He told her his mom's house was a zoo right now, with sisters and brothers dividing everything that was left.

"They all get along pretty good. No fighting. Mom wouldn't have stood for it." He sighed. "Guess it's a good thing we never got ahold of Brenda Lee. She'd have stirred things up in a hurry."

Helen chuckled, thinking how hard their task would be if Haley had decided to stick around.

"I got the two things I wanted—a picture and the afghan Mom was making for Brenda Lee." Pudge shifted in his seat. "'Spect we'd better get back to work."

"I'm going to The Boulder to grab a bite," she announced three days later. "Want me to bring you a sandwich?"

Helen wasn't sure how she'd get everything done before she flew back to New York the next morning, but she did want to make time for lunch and a piece of pie.

"That's okay. I brought my lunch," Pudge called over the country music hum of his radio. "But thanks."

She liked the chemistry that had developed between them during the last three days.

"He seems to sense what needs to be done first," she told Mrs. Lochschmidt, who'd decided to join her in a booth after she'd said goodbye to a well-dressed man in a business suit. "Pudge is an amazing worker, in spite of having to deal with the pain of losing his mom."

"And his job to boot." Mrs. Lochschmidt sipped her coffee and craned her neck to see if the obvious out-of-towner had left the building. Satisfied that he'd fired up his expensive car, she fixed her eyes on Helen.

"Who is that guy—the one in the suit?" Helen scolded herself for sounding like a nosy local yokel, but she was curious. The well-groomed man in his crisp business attire didn't fit in here—like one of Haley's Ken dolls in the middle of a collection of Raggedy Anns.

"A fellow who stops in here on his way to Danville." Mrs. Lochschmidt waved her hand to dismiss Helen's question, eager to return to their original topic. "Pudge finished everything I could find for him, so I'm glad you've got him for the duration. All them Simpkins kids, you know, were raised to work hard."

"He told me a lot about his family." Helen savored a bite of her toasted chicken salad on sourdough and wondered why nobody in Manhattan seemed to be able to make a simple sandwich this tasty. But nobody in Manhattan would consider sitting down, uninvited, with a customer dining alone. Helen realized she couldn't wait to get back to the city and its crackling energy. And her privacy. Her blessed privacy. One week of life in Rockwell's slow lane and its countless prying citizens was all she could take.

"And if you stayed on, he'd prob'ly tell you a lot more." Mrs. Lochschmidt straightened the condiments at the end of the table. "Fayetta and Henry ran a tight ship, but in that house there was never a dull moment. Too bad you have to hurry back east."

"Duty calls," Helen explained. "Deadlines and a special anniversary issue we're working on. My desk will be piled sky high." She wanted to add that she missed Burt but didn't want to open the door to let Mrs. Lochschmidt into that corner of her life.

"Well, it's good you can pop in on your dad once in awhile. Guess your sister's too busy." Mrs. Lochschmidt's observation seemed more like a question.

"I'm going to visit him later this afternoon." Helen sighed. "It's hard though, seeing him the way he is now."

"He was always your buddy." Mrs. Lochschmidt paused as she remembered. "While the rest of the town was fussin' over Haley, your dad'd take you out someplace. To the drugstore. To the newsstand. Just the two of you."

"He made me feel import—" The words stalled over

a lump in her throat. She took a drink of water and hoped Mrs. Lochschmidt hadn't noticed. "Important," she finished lamely. A wave of homesickness washed over her. She missed her dad, the way he'd been when she was growing up. And she missed New York. This time tomorrow, she thought with relief, she'd be in a cab on her way to her apartment.

"Nice seeing you again, Mrs. Lochschmidt," she said pleasantly as she picked up her bill and headed for the cash register. "I'll be back late in the spring."

"Next time you see me let's drop the formal stuff, okay? I want you to call me Doris." The older woman winked. "After all, that's my name."

"You've got it . . . Doris."

Outside, she felt a sense of peace as a few snowflakes dusted her cheeks. Eager to complete her to-do list before she left, she pointed "Black Beauty" toward the house.

Once there, everything seemed to take twice as long as it should. Pudge wanted a written list of directions in the order she'd like the work completed. Feeling rushed, she was upset with herself for forgetting to do her online check-in for her flight and dismayed when she learned she'd be in the last group boarding. By the time she reached Happy Haven at 4:15, she found that an aide had already taken her dad to his eating station. Lord, she thought, people in New York were now finishing their lunch.

She always tried to avoid Happy Haven at mealtime. It seemed to be the worst of all worlds—former vibrant community leaders now wearing large bibs and nestled into their wheel chairs at tables for four. But since she was late, she pulled up a spare chair and sat beside her father while an aide spooned small globs of a colorless mushy entree into his sagging mouth. Unable to watch, she gazed around the room and spotted several feeble folks whose splashy country club parties had been the pinnacle of her parents' social life. Glancing out the window, she was surprised to see heavy snow swirling in the beam of a light in the parking lot. Still, in spite of all her good intentions to leave early, she lingered and watched the evening game shows with her dad. When she pulled on her coat, he squeezed her hand and managed a lopsided grin.

"Night, Dad," she whispered as she kissed his forehead.

She was shocked by the bite of the wind that peppered her face with icy pellets. Feeling the frigid slush seep into her shoes, she wished she had worn boots. By the time she reached the car, her socks were soaked.

She couldn't believe the weight of the snow that she scraped from her windows with her long-handled brush. Finally, she decided to start the car and use the blower to melt the layer of ice underneath. Impatient to get back to the house, she revved the engine, shifted into reverse, and backed up cautiously. As she inched her way toward the highway bordering Happy Haven, she was shocked when she skidded to a stop.

Damn, she thought, why did I stay for Dad's dinner? I should have been out of here an hour ago. She yearned for Manhattan, where cabs and subways were at her disposal. A pickup zipped past, hurling slush against her windshield as it overtook her.

"Ass," she growled. Refusing to let some hotshot make her look like an old fogey, she bore down on the accelerator.

As she squinted through the blizzard to make sure she didn't miss her right turn onto Main Street, she neglected to see the snow plow approaching on her left.

She had no idea she'd wandered into its path. The screech of the giant machine, the scrunch of her own tires on the pavement, the awful grinding of metal squashing metal were the last sounds she heard before she realized a crew had come to lift her onto a stretcher and load her into an ambulance.

She tasted salt—blood, maybe—and felt someone applying pressure to her left cheek. Bright overhead lights prevented her from opening her eyes, but the antiseptic smell that pierced each breath told her she must be in a hospital. Muffled phrases from urgent voices sifted through the ball of cotton that occupied her brain—"sedate, stabilize arm and leg, check her purse for ID and someone to call." The searing pain that tore through her left leg and arm blocked her from saying, "Burt . . . New York . . . Burt . . ."

She was a prisoner, anchored onto something that kept her from moving, yet somehow comforted by the smell of freshly scrubbed sheets. Had her mother done the laundry that day? And why was she confined to bed? Had she misbehaved? Was her mother punishing her again?

"Sorry," she mumbled. Maybe if she apologized for whatever offense she'd committed, her mother would allow her to curl up behind her favorite overstuffed chair in the corner of the parlor and browse through the pages of *Flat*

Stanley. Maybe if she made herself as skinny as Stanley, she could slide right out of whatever was holding her down. "Sorry," she repeated.

"You've got nothing to be sorry about." A woman's weary voice reassured her. She felt a hand hardened by years of work cover hers. "You got tangled up with a snow plow, honey. Rest easy and let us take care of you."

"Sorry . . ." she replied.

During the next day she tried to piece together the events that had brought her to this place, but her brain kept tripping over the information. Something terrible had happened to her left side. The pain told her that much.

"But nothing life-threatening," said Dr. Patel, the orthopod who came from Champaign to Rockwell twice a week. "We will take care of your broken arm and leg. We can do that here."

"Broken arm <u>and</u> leg?" No wonder she felt so crappy.

"Yes." In his crisp accent, he outlined her other injuries. "You also have some ligament damage in your ankle. And a couple of broken ribs."

"Shit."

"We will need to do an ORIF on the two broken bones in your leg. I've scheduled that for day after tomorrow."

"What the hell is that?" She felt her lips rebel as she forced out the thick words.

"An open reduction internal fixation." His brown eyes softened. "You are lucky to be here at all, you know. If you

97

are a good patient and follow your rehab schedule, you should be almost good as new in six weeks or so."

"Six weeks?" she yelped. "I don't have that kind of time to do nothing."

"Ah, what your arm and leg need most is time. Time for healing." He placed his hand gently on her right arm. "I fix it up, you take care of it, and all will be well."

Once her pain was under control, she attempted to work through the wall of fuzz in her head. Wasn't she supposed to be flying to LaGuardia?

"No prob," a twenty-something aide with a butterfly tattoo on her wrist told her. "Some red-haired guy came in real early this morning. He took responsibility for you. Said you had a friend in New York who could cancel your flight."

Pudge? Burt? The idea of the two of them communicating without her made her head hurt. Again, she drifted off to a place where her dad was pulling her on a sled across snow-covered sidewalks in their neighborhood. "Whee!" she squealed. "Whoopee!" From a faraway place she could hear the aide giggle.

Her first glimpse of normalcy came that afternoon when Pudge appeared at the end of her bed.

"Hey." His pale face was etched in concern.

"Hey yourself." The energy required to propel words out of her mouth made her close her eyes again. "What happened?"

In her self-imposed darkness she heard Pudge say she'd sideswiped a snowplow and been "hurt pretty bad."

"Good thing you were in your dad's big old car or you'd 've been a goner. Doc said so."

She groaned when he repeated the same information she'd heard from Dr. Patel. She'd hoped it had all been a bad dream.

"Lord." She winced as she moved a few inches.

"Doc said he'll do surgery on your leg in a couple of days. He's gonna wait to decide if you'll need it on your arm but he doesn't think so."

"But—"

"I know, I know. You've gotta get back to work. And you will. Just not today."

"But—"

"Hush, now. It'll be okay."

She soon learned that "just not today" meant at least six to eight weeks before she could even think about making the trip to New York. Her immediate decision involved whether she wanted to be transferred to rehab in Danville for three weeks or return to her house, hire a caregiver, and have daily in-home therapy.

"Lucky for you you've already got that ramp," Pudge reminded her the day after her surgery. He handed her a cup of water with a bendy straw.

"That's at least one good thing that came out of my mom's Parkinson's." She grimaced as the tepid water trickled down her throat. "And we do have that downstairs bathroom with the walk-in shower. It even has a seat and grab bar. Mom used that while she could still bathe herself."

Pudge studied her thoughtfully.

"I'll be at your house every day."

She could tell he was thinking out loud. Closing her eyes, she pictured herself in a sterile, unfamiliar room in a rehab facility in Danville, where staff members constantly tried to motivate her.

"Shit." She sighed.

"You don't want me there?" Pudge's face looked as if she'd slapped him.

"No, no, Pudge. Don't mind me. I was thinking about the rehab in Danville."

"I bet me'n Kristi could take care of you. She worked as an aide at Happy Haven a few years ago before she got her job at the school." He pushed his hand through his hair. "Let me talk with her and see what she thinks."

"You're crazy, you know?" She managed a weak smile.

"Always have been." His grin revealed the signature Simpkins gap. "You ask somebody around here what equipment you'll need and you may not have to go to Danville."

She felt her eyes closing again. When she opened them, late afternoon shadows were creeping across her room, and the cheery aide with the butterfly tattoo announced that she'd come to crank up the bed for supper.

The next morning, a male nurse said he would help her move to a chair.

"Don't wanta," she protested.

"Got to." There wasn't an ounce of sympathy in his tone-less voice that sounded like a robot straight out of a bad science-fiction movie.

Later that day, after her pain medication had taken effect, a stocky silver-haired woman with a clipboard entered her room.

"I'm Vickie, your discharge nurse," she stated with authority as she settled herself into the chair next to Helen's bed. "Came to tell you what's going to happen so you can make some choices, okay?" Over her clipboard her bright blue eyes scrutinized Helen. "You'll be here for a few days with Jake helping you. Then you can go to the rehab in Danville and everything you need'll be right there. You won't have a worry in the world."

"Okay." Helen thought her own voice sounded strained and remote. She cleared her throat.

"But if you decide to go home, you'll have to rent a hospital bed and toilet and have help 24-7. I could talk with Dr. Patel about ordering a platform attachment for your walker that'd allow your weight to be transferred to your upper left arm. That way you could get around without damaging your lower arm, okay?"

"Okay." Lord, as she tried to picture herself, she could only imagine a robot with all kinds of gadgets hanging from her.

"Tell you what. You think about it and let me know in a few days. Doesn't have to be tomorrow." For a chunky woman, Vickie was amazingly nimble as she popped up from the chair. Helen wondered if she would ever be that spry again.

Vickie turned as she reached the door.

"I know this sounds like an awful lot. Me'n you—we're probably about the same age, and things take us longer." She focused her blue eyes on Helen and telegraphed a look of compassion and confidence. "But I think you can make it. And if I think you can make it, you will. Okay?"

"Okay," Helen echoed. Lord, she thought, how could I be in a worse place? She gave great consideration to that question before she recalled Pudge's reminder that "Black Beauty" had saved her life. As her eyes began to shut again, she was thankful in some weird way that her dad would never realize his beloved Cadillac had been totaled and would be dismantled for parts.

Pudge

He wasn't sure he was the right man for this job. "Wrong guy . . . wrong time . . . wrong place." He tossed a stack of moth-eaten wool blankets into the throw-away pile that swallowed up more than its share of space in the Hamilton attic.

Shoot, he wondered, wouldn't it make more sense for him to be helping with his mom's things now instead of cleaning out someone else's junk? But no, his sisters had assured him they could zip right through their mom's house and that Helen Hamilton needed him more than they did. Whatever.

Maybe, he mused, this was easier 'cause he had no feelings for any of it. He opened several dusty boxes of check stubs from 1974 to 1979 and set them beside the blankets. Next came an album of family photos. As he thumbed through it, he realized most of them were of Haley with her baton and sequined twirling costume and Haley in her high-school cheerleader's uniform. In one picture, she was posing with a bright smile as she placed a saucer of milk in front of a kitten. Off to the side stood a large girl with straight hair.

He squinted to take a closer look. Must be Helen, he thought. Poor plain Helen, always at the edge of the picture.

As he unearthed boxes of photos, he was struck with the thought that his mom had only a handful of pictures of their family. They hadn't owned a camera and couldn't afford film anyway. Then when he was in third grade, his sister Patsy had won a Kodak for selling magazines to raise money for her class prom. The whole family couldn't have been more excited if they'd been given a trip to Niagara Falls or somewhere. His older sisters and brothers with part-time jobs vowed to donate a little from their weekly earnings to the film fund.

Suddenly overcome with memories, he felt his legs wobble and sank down on the stack of musty blankets. He remembered the fun his family had with that camera, sneaking up on each other to take wacky shots. His mom had laughed so hard at some of those pictures she'd almost wet her pants. These people in most of the Hamilton family photos looked like mannequins pretending to be happy.

Pudge felt tears spill down his cheeks at the thought of how much his mom enjoyed her kids. For the first time since he'd found her in her chair, he buried his head in his hands and sobbed. He wept for the lively family years that were gone forever and for the lost job that had been his lifeblood. And finally, when he thought he'd used up all his tears, he cried for Helen, who'd been given so much and yet had so little.

That evening in the kitchen as he and Kristi dawdled over the last pieces of cake from the funeral dinner, he tried to share his feelings about Helen with his wife.

"I mean, you look around that attic and see all that stuff. Old Walt must have inherited a bundle and Helen's mom had to have come from rich people. Looks like St. Louis from the pictures I've seen." He ran his fork around his plate to capture the last crumbs of funeral cake. "But Kristi, think of those two girls. Haley's a lot like our Brenda Lee. And it seems like—well, it seems like Helen got nothin'."

"So sad." Kristi shook her head as she scooped up their plates and set them in the sink. "And now she's stuck here for six weeks, right?"

"With nobody. Absolutely nobody." He sighed.

"Let me think about that." She swished their plates through the suds, rinsed them, and set them in the drainer.

He glanced at his wife and realized she was chewing her lip like she always did when she was concentrating.

"You know," she began, "Jenna and I could take turns staying evenings and nights with her." She scoured the pasta pan as she went through the scenario out loud. "You'll be there all day." She stopped to scrape a stubborn string of spaghetti from the bottom of the kettle. "She'll have to be able to take care of herself in the bathroom before they'll ever let her out of the hospital. I know that for a fact."

"Are you saying . . ." He was almost afraid to hope that Kristi had come up with a plan before he'd had a chance to suggest one.

"Yes, I'm saying the three of us could cover that for six weeks." She stopped rinsing the pan and fixed her eyes on him. "But only if that's what she wants." She nodded to agree with her own statement. "Only if that's what she really wants."

For the first time in weeks, he smiled to himself and wondered how he'd he been lucky enough to land a wife who knew what he was thinking before he did. He sure was glad he'd shared his worries with her.

Helen

Never had her mind been so busy and her body so use-less. She stared at the melting snow that dripped silently from the branches of the stately oak tree outside her hospital window and tried to ignore the inane chatter that streamed from the television.

Her brain buzzed with concern over the mountain of work she should be attacking in New York. Deadlines for articles that demanded meticulous editing loomed ahead for the big anniversary issue. Several guest writers had submit-ted essays praising the unique flavor of *The Arch*, but she'd learned the hard way that the most famous authors often required the most scrutiny. Seymour Applegate continued to sell thousands of books but still didn't recognize a dangling participle when he wrote one. Maybe that afternoon she'd try to call her boss.

"Time for your vitals, honey." An aide cheerfully popped a thermometer under Helen's tongue and checked her pulse and blood pressure. "Lookin' good." Although the girl's cranberry hair and blond bangs made Helen's eyes hurt, she managed a weak smile.

"They'll be shippin' you outta here in a few days. But you need to start eatin' better." The aide's nasal tone bored into the core of Helen's headache. "Any idea if you'll be goin' to rehab or gettin' a caregiver at home?"

"Not yet." Lord, she felt thirsty. And tired.

"I got a cousin who might be able to come over and stay at your house." The aide straightened her bedding. "She's a hoot. You and her could watch all the game shows and soaps on TV together. D'ya like 'The Young And The Restless?' My cousin never misses it."

Helen closed her eyes, refusing to waste energy on a response. When she opened them again, the aide was gone. She sighed and turned her attention to the snow that continued to melt from charcoal branches against a leaden sky.

When Malcolm Overmyer called from New York early that afternoon, he assured her he wasn't going to allow her to wiggle out of her responsibilities. *The Arch* needed her. Although his tone was gruff when he stated she could work from a laptop wherever she was, she detected an underlying concern in his voice. Somehow, she marveled, this old curmudgeon had managed to lift her spirits more than any of her medications.

A few moments later, when Burt checked in for their daily phone chat, he reported he and Miss Adelaide were getting along famously, although the "damn cat" demanded an inordinate amount of attention. After Helen chuckled, he confessed he'd taken his nephew to see *Picnic*. The show hadn't been that great, he added.

Every person she knew, including Dr. Patel, tried to remind her there was a real life waiting for her. Still, she continued to berate herself for lingering at the nursing home the night of the accident. If only she'd left before her dad's supper. Her head throbbed from the endless string of "if only" scenarios that haunted her.

She shifted her focus to the future and considered her options: Rehab vs. Home. Each time she pictured herself in Danville, she saw her body as another piece of meat, devoid of all identity, manhandled by strangers in a facility stripped of any warmth. However, if she returned to the familiar surroundings of her family home, she'd be staying in an aging house she never liked, in a town she always hated, with some tattooed twit to help her. It was all too much. She felt herself drifting off to sleep again.

Strange, Helen thought in a foggy state that she found herself seated amid her family members who were ordering a meal at The Boulder. Haley was whining because she couldn't have a soda for brunch. Their mother, Gilda, looked young and fit as she anxiously scanned the room for anyone who might catch her slumming at this ordinary restaurant. After all, everyone knew that Gilda Hamilton much preferred the atmosphere of the coffee nook tucked into a corner of Just For Her, the only Rockwell shop that offered trendy clothes plus the latest wicked gossip. Her dad was geared in on what he should order.

Frustrated, Helen knew she smelled French toast but couldn't find it on the menu. Aching from head to toe, she moaned as she tried to get comfortable in the blue vinyl booth.

"It's a bitch. I know I've been there."

When she peeked through slitted eyes and saw Doris Lochschmidt had pulled up a chair, Helen realized she'd been dreaming. The aromas of home cooking embedded deep into the fuzzy slate-blue wool of Doris's winter coat had invaded the hospital room. No wonder she thought she was in The Boulder.

"Brought you something to ease the pain." Her visitor dug into her tote, whipped out a small plastic triangle, and placed it on the bed table. "Coconut cream pie. Made it this morning and saved a piece for you." Her worn face relaxed into a maze of wrinkles as she smiled. "There's nothin' better for healin' than a good slice of pie."

"Thank you." Her words came hard—wooden things that stuck to the roof of her mouth. "I'm so tired—"

"That's why I wanted to see you. And I can't stay long." Doris draped her coat over the back of the chair and began her tale. She shared the story of the wreck she'd been in five years before when Dougie's boat rammed a steel pier in the dark on Lake Michigan. "Twasn't his fault," she added protectively.

Helen began to understand the weariness this woman had experienced during her own recovery and the elation she must have felt when she graduated from "that damn walker" to the cane. "Everyone wondered if I'd make it. But I showed 'em." Helen felt Doris pat her good arm through the bedding. "And you will too."

She cringed at the thought of what "making it" would entail and the prospect of boarding a subway when she returned to New York. "Sometimes I don't think—"

"You will. If I could do it at my age, you can too. And you know what? I can still do some decent cookin' when I need to." Doris paused and leaned closer. "Don't tell anybody, but that funeral dinner 'bout wore me out."

"Pudge's mom?" Helen shifted her focus from her own pain to Pudge's ordeal. "What an awful thing. First, his job then his mom—"

"Me'n Fayetta—that's his mom—went all through Sweet Briar together. Then both of us got pregnant before we was ready and had to quit school."

Helen digested this information. She'd never known that this mainstay of Rockwell's business section had to get married.

"Fayetta and Henry had more kids'n I did. Nine altogether." Doris paused as she remembered. "You never seen such a big funeral!"

"I'm glad for Pudge." Helen thought of the man who was sorting through the mounds of keepsakes in her attic and wondered how he had survived the last two weeks.

"Friends. Relatives. They came out of the woodwork. Fayetta would've been bowled over."

Helen tried to picture the scene as Doris described it. The crew from The Boulder had cooked chicken and noodles plus meatloaf for two hundred, "like they predicted, but musta been closer to three hundred there."

Helen watched Doris come alive as she related how her

workers decided to dole out portions on each paper plate; otherwise, "they'd have cleaned us out before half of 'em got served." She chuckled at the picture Doris painted of "them Baptist ladies cutting some pretty skimpy slices of pie and cake to make sure everybody got some." Then she held her breath when Doris grew quiet, picked a piece of lint from her black slacks, and finally confessed that she hadn't been able to talk about her memories of Fayetta when the sharing time came.

"Just plain froze up and couldn't say hardly a word. Felt kinda stupid in front of all those people."

"I bet you did fine." Helen asked Doris to push the button to raise her bed a little and hand her the piece of pie. When she bit into it and reveled in the flaky pastry bursting with sweet, smooth filling, she felt she, too, might rejoin the human race.

"So, so good," she said, her mouth full.

Slipping into her coat, Doris beamed.

"Glad you like it. It'll give you some energy for that rotten rehab they're gonna put you through."

Helen nodded ruefully.

"And me?" Her visitor's eyes revealed a deep weariness as they looked directly into hers. "I'm goin' home to take a nap. A good funeral can sure wear a person out. For days."

The next morning when Dr. Patel discussed her rehab program, Helen was surprised to see Pudge shadowing him.

"Hello there, young lady. How's my beautiful patient

today?" Lord, she hated it when her surgeon started every conversation that way. After all, she was probably old enough to be his mother and twice as ugly. "We need to talk about sending you off to Danville for your rehab program."

When the doctor paused to check his cell, Pudge grabbed the opportunity.

"If that's where you really want to go." His earnest gaze was warm, but he sounded hesitant.

"Me 'n Kristi—well, like I told you, we'll be glad to help you out. If you want us to."

"What this young man is trying to say is that he and his wife will supervise your care." Dr. Patel slid his cell out of the pocket of his jacket and checked a text. "You need to be positively sure that if you decide to accept his offer, you have everything you need in your own home."

"You mean—" she fumbled for words. "I wouldn't have to—" She tried to grasp what Dr. Patel was saying. "I could—"

"This fellow has talked with me about your rehab and explained how he and his wife could take care of you at home. Of course, we'd have you brought to the hospital for periodic checkups, but if I order the equipment you need, I see no reason why his plan wouldn't work." Dr. Patel rubbed the dark stubble on his chin as he watched her reaction.

"I'll be at your house every day anyway. I'll make sure you do everything they want you to do." Pudge blurted out his plan faster than she'd ever heard him speak. "And Kristi was a night aide at Happy Haven when we was first married. She knows about all that stuff. Her and our daughter, Jenna, can take turns staying nights."

Helen wondered if she were dreaming once more. If she could recuperate in a hospital bed at home, she could avoid the entire sterile, impersonal environment of rehab. She could escape from the clutches of Jake, the grim therapist who'd started her rehab and rest when she wanted to. Listen quietly to her own thoughts. Start to work—uninterrupted by rehab personnel—on her laptop. And feel like a real person again. She glanced from Dr. Patel, whose clinical countenance was impassive, to Pudge, whose face was hopeful.

"Only if you want to." Pudge assured her. "It's your choice."

"We'll need to talk about your pay," she ventured. "And Kristi's too, of course."

"You two work out the details. I'll start the orders for what you'll need at home." Dr. Patel, eager to continue his rounds, paused in the doorway. "You know, you're pretty lucky to have family who can do this for you."

Helen nodded in agreement, overcome with the emotion welling up inside her. As she and Pudge looked at each other, they began to chuckle at Dr. Patel's error. Family? Both were so amused that they snickered, then snorted out loud. Oh Lord, it hurt to laugh, but did it ever feel good!

"Family?" She tossed the question to Pudge. "I should be that lucky."

When he grinned back at her, she added softly, "And maybe I am."

Monty

"Corporate wants definite recommendations in ten days. NO LATER!"

Monty scowled when he read Gordon Strunke's insistent memo that took top billing over the other demands stacked on his desk. Who did Strunke think Monty was—a miracle worker? Did the guy have any idea how long it took to collect and compile data on five possible new locations?

He scanned his schedule for the day and reluctantly decided to skip the Chamber lunch. That would free up enough time for Al and him to come up with a recommendation that would keep Strunke at bay for a few days. He asked his secretary to call Al and tell him to come to Monty's office. They'd order sandwiches from Mullen's later.

"Dammit." He hated it when one element of his well-ordered life pre-empted another. He'd looked forward to the Chamber meeting so he could volunteer to head up the downtown landscaping committee. He knew he was the perfect person for that job but realized that right now, he'd better keep focused on his work.

He gazed from his fourth-floor window and wished his

life were flowing as smoothly as the traffic on I-88. But right now he felt as if each person he knew was pressuring him for a top-notch performance every single day.

"Dammit!" he exclaimed again when a call from Claire interrupted his train of thought. He hadn't slept well after their disagreement over a prospective new home. He was furious with Fiona Fentress, head of the dance company board, for telling Claire that they might have a chance of grabbing a prime property in Barrington if they called the realtor right away. And, although he'd gobbled a handful of antacids, he stayed awake wondering why his wife couldn't be content with what they had.

"What's up?" he barked into the phone.

"Well hello to you too." Claire's honeyed tones warned him that she wanted something.

"Sorry. Got a business thing going here."

"Me too. Listen to this." She gushed the news that the realtor for the Barrington house could meet them there at 4:30 that afternoon. "I think we've got the inside track, Monty."

He stared at his phone in disbelief. What the hell did the two of them want with the "inside track" on any house in Barrington?

"I've got a meeting with the 'Y' tonight. And traffic's terrible at that hour. You know that."

"And I also know this place could slip away if we don't go. Today. At 4:30. You've got the address, Cooper. I'll see you there." The cell went dead.

Irritably he studied his Day-Timer. If he and Al could confer from noon until 1:30 over lunch and he could reschedule his 3:30 meeting with Human Resources about health insurance, he guessed he could make it to Barrington by 4:30. But only for half an hour. He'd promised himself he would get to the "Y" meeting tonight, and dammit, he was going to do it. When the realtor's tour of the cavernous mansion took fifty-five minutes instead of thirty, Monty was too harried to have a sit-down meal at home. Still, it had been worth the extra time to see Claire blanch when she heard the absolute lowest offer the owner would entertain was $300,000 over their budget. He grinned as he spread peanut butter between two slices of sourdough and grabbed a banana to eat in the car.

On his way out the door, he spotted Theo coming down from his room.

"I need to talk with you about summer plans," Monty called over his shoulder to his son. "Tomorrow evening."

As he made a mental note to pencil that appointment into his Day-Timer, he heard his son grumble, "Whatever."

That seemed to be Theo's standard response to everything these days, Monty realized as he fired up his car. Wolfing down half of his sandwich, he turned at his corner and vowed he'd straighten out some differences between the two of them. For one thing, he'd let his son know he could go to the ballet camp at Aspen in July but only if he attended the weeklong basketball camp at Northwestern in June. That was the leverage he'd use. As he parked at the "Y," he congratulated himself on being able to apply some of his management skills to get the results he wanted from his family.

The next day Monty felt himself relax as each piece of his plan fell neatly into place. After his invigorating morning swim, he met with Al to finalize their evaluations of the possible sites for the new GRN location. Gordon Strunke seemed pleased when Monty personally delivered them to him.

That evening he tried to ignore Claire's sulkiness while they dined on rotisserie chicken and deli salads. Her disappointment over the Barrington house was palpable, but secretly he was relieved that—at least for the immediate future—this place would continue to be their home. He agreed with her the time would come when they'd need a more prestigious location, but right now they'd dodged the financial bullet of a massive mortgage.

After dinner he strode into Theo's room and tried to overlook the ballet garbage that covered the walls.

"Got a deal for you." Monty knew his teaser sounded like a used car salesman, but he had to grab his son's attention.

Stretched out the full length of his bed, Theo loosened his ear buds and studied him warily.

"How'd you like to go to Aspen?" He watched as his son's suspicion turned to disbelief. Theo stood and looked him in the eye.

"Really?" His son's face was cautiously hopeful. "You're not shittin' me—"

"Theo!" Monty chided him gently. "If that's what you want to do, that's what you'll get to do."

"Dad! I don't know what to say—"

"One condition, son. If you sign up for Aspen in July, you'll need to go to basketball camp at Northwestern in June."

Monty's words hung between them, erasing the joy from Theo's face.

"But I don't want—"

Monty raised his hand, signaling for silence. "That's the deal." He was shocked at the misery his son displayed. "You'll be grateful to me later. Believe me."

Theo muttered something indiscernible. His shoulders drooped as he stared at the Chicago Bulls quilt he'd had since he was eight.

"What'd you say?" Monty would have no insolence.

"Nothing." Theo sighed. He stood, squaring his shoulders to remind Monty he was now an inch taller. "If that's what I have to do, I'll take the deal. Anything else?"

Monty studied his son's impassive face. "Guess not."

"Whatever."

There it was again. That word, the only blemish on a perfect transaction. Still, satisfied Theo would get to basketball camp, Monty hummed a few bars of "Take the 'A' Train" and headed down the stairs. That was the beauty of a plan. You made it. You worked it into your schedule. And you executed it.

If only that poor red-haired guy back at the restaurant in Rockwell had learned that principle, he might be in control of his own life too. Monty wondered if he should talk with him about it if they had the opportunity. He'd really like to be able to show him how careful organization in a person's life could put him in the driver's seat.

Glancing at his watch, he saw he had twenty minutes before NOVA started. He might even check out the following PBS program on successful leaders in America.

"Anyone want to get a frozen custard?" If they hurried, it would be nice to squeeze in some family time before his favorite show.

No one answered.

"Claire?"

"No, that's okay. Take the kids."

He shrugged. "Cass? A double dipper?"

"I'm good." His daughter fiddled with her cell.

Knowing he needn't ask Theo, he wandered alone into the den and tuned in PBS. His show would be on in a few minutes anyway.

Doris

March

Whack! Cherisse lowered the knife with confidence and cubed the potatoes to the perfect size.

"You're gettin' to be some kind of expert. Know that?" Doris gazed fondly at her great-granddaughter as the two worked together in The Boulder kitchen. People sure didn't call Cherisse "Little Doris" for nothin'.

"Grando." Cherisse scolded her patiently. "I've been doing this since I was ten."

"Well, you're growin' up too fast. Sometimes at night—" she paused to reflect on the great-grandchildren who shared her home and enriched her life—"I let Nettie and Emmy climb up on my lap while Cory turns the pages of the story I'm readin'. And I realize they'll all be grown up like you in the blink of an eye."

Doris sighed and considered this fact of life for a moment, then continued to line two large roasters and a smaller one with foil for the Polish dinner she and Cherisse were preparing. She hoped the Saturday-night special would draw a crowd on such a cold night. March sure was coming in like a lion.

"Why are we making the extra one, Grando?"

Doris grinned. Nothing much seemed to slip past Cherisse.

"Gonna take one over to Helen Hamilton's. She's back in her own house now." Doris covered the kielbasa with a cabbage and tomato mixture and began to top it off with Cherisse's potatoes.

"The lady who ran into the snow plow a while back?" Cherisse chopped the last potato and laid the large knife in the sink.

"Yep."

"How's she gonna eat all that?" Cherisse eyed the smaller roaster. "It'll take her a week."

"Not with Pudge and Kristi and their kids. They're all helpin' her out. Won't take long for them to make short work of this."

Cherisse popped a piece of raw potato into her mouth. "What're they doing there? Doesn't she have any family around?"

"Her dad's out at Happy Haven. Helen came here to help <u>him</u>. Her shit-for-brains twin sister Haley was here last fall but took off after a few days. She'd be no use in a situation like this anyway." Doris snorted. "Pudge was able to get in touch with her, and all Haley could say was she guessed it would take a while longer to get the house ready to sell. Can you believe that? Never a word about her sister bein' all banged up." She shook her head at the thought of Haley Hamilton and continued to place potatoes around the edge of each roaster.

"So now you get the picture." She rinsed her hands and dried them. "Pudge needed a job real bad, with Midwest closin' and all. He's been workin' days at Helen's house, and his wife 'n daughter are stayin' nights till Helen can move around better."

"They're all going to love this, Grando. Got any dessert for them?"

Doris grinned. She liked Cherisse's way of thinking. "Made a pie before you got here. And later, when I take everything to Helen's, I want you to go with me to help carry it in. Got any plans late this afternoon?"

"Nope."

When Cherisse glanced aside, Doris knew what was missing. Friends—that was it. She wished her great-granddaughter had a pack of pals like the old Fearless Four. They'd been the best thing in Doris's life when she was Cherisse's age, would've done anything for each other. But Cherisse had always been so wrapped up in NASCAR that other girls shied away from her. She'd limited herself to three pastimes—hanging out at The Boulder, following NASCAR, and scribbling God-knows-what in that notebook she kept at home. Doris sighed, wondering if she could figure out a way to help Cherisse crawl out of her shell.

"There. The oven's pre-heated and ready for these roasters. Help me get 'em in the oven so this place'll start smellin' good enough to make the lunch customers wanta come back for supper."

Cherisse smiled back at her. Honest-to-god, Doris thought, it's like lookin' into my own face when I was her age. If that girl didn't have black hair, I'd swear I'd been cloned.

Helen

She'd thought she'd be relieved to be back at her house. Instead, fingers of uncertainty and anger crept into each moment of every day, especially when Jolly Jake, the Torture Master, followed her. She'd assumed he'd remain at the hospital to tighten the screws on a whole new crop of rehab patients; yet, here he was—bossing her around in her own house.

She resented the very sight of this muscle-bound guy with pale blue eyes and shaved head who demanded she complete impossible tasks. Worse yet was the sound of his upbeat tenor voice that explained in thin tones what he was doing with her bad leg and how it might hurt "just a bit."

Hurt? Hell, Jake was damn near killing her and all the time wearing that tight little smile. He was a sadist in disguise—that's what he was, his services approved by some nameless twisted insurance employee hundreds of miles away. She wondered if the company realized they'd hired a guy who delighted in punishing people.

Her chipper visiting nurse who stopped in twice a week

was equally as irritating, ending every sentence like a question:

"Bet you're glad to be back in your own home?"
"We'll check on your pain medication dosage?"
"They say we may get another blizzard tonight?"

Worse yet, the forty-something man from the medical supply company who came to make sure all her rental equipment was working gave her the creeps. After she'd seen him the first day when he slithered into her room with his lank black hair clinging to his acne-scarred face, she always pretended to be asleep when he arrived. She hoped never to share a snippet of conversation with him as he checked her hospital bed, wheel chair, and all the gizmos Dr. Patel and Jake had ordered. When she heard him humming the same tuneless melody each time he visited, she wondered if she'd been dropped into the middle of a horror movie.

She understood that all these members of her medical team were only doing their jobs, but Lord, they were annoying! They made her want to embrace Pudge and his family for the simple and silent way they cared for her.

Each morning she welcomed Pudge when he arrived as the winter sun was shooting its first pale rays through the faded draperies. Within minutes he delivered freshly brewed coffee and warm buttered toast that he'd made in her kitchen, then cranked up her bed so she could check her laptop before the medical pros began to pester her.

Her spirits were lifted every day when her new friends sailed through her front door with sprightly

"Yoo-hoos"—Doris, who brought chicken salad sandwiches and pie two or three times a week; Kristi and Jenna, who took turns sleeping at the house; and Cherisse, who frequently joined her for supper.

Helen knew in her heart that Doris must have bribed Cherisse to join her; no fourteen-year-old in her right mind would have volunteered. The first night, their sparse conversation had been stilted, but Cherisse's interest perked up when Helen showed her an online manuscript she was correcting.

"See this guy here?" Helen handed her laptop to Cherisse. "He's a great writer—one of the best. But sometimes he gets all tangled up in his words, uses way too many. And his grammar can be off, especially if he's been writing when he's drunk."

Cherisse giggled. "Doesn't he get mad when you change his stuff?"

"Oh, yeah. But then he reads my edits, reads his original paragraphs, reads the edits again and agrees. He can be pretty grumpy. But he's okay."

Cherisse was quiet as she examined the screen. "So this is what you do for a living?"

"Yep." With effort, Helen placed the laptop back on the bed beside her. "It's kind of an invisible job—you know, like a seamstress who makes a dress fit better. I've always liked working with words."

"Me too." When Cherisse's gray eyes met hers, Helen felt a connection. "Did—well, did other kids ever think you were weird? You know, treat you like you were a nerd?"

Helen's laughter erupted. "Oh, kiddo, did they ever! I

was always on the outside looking in."

"Me too."

When Helen saw the sadness in her young friend's eyes, she had an idea.

"Tell you what," Helen said. "You like to write. And I like to read. Correct?"

Cherisse nodded.

"Then why don't you bring me something you've written so I can read it?"

Cherisse hung her head. "I'd be too embarrassed."

"Not if I showed you some of the things I wrote at your age." Helen sensed the fragility of the girl at her bedside. "In fact, if you want, you can tell me what was wrong with <u>my</u> stuff. How does that sound?"

"Pretty funny." A smile played at the edges of Cherisse's mouth.

"But we won't tell anyone, right?" Trust between them would be imperative, Helen knew.

"Okay." Cherisse sounded hesitant.

"Deal?" Helen stuck out her hand.

"Deal." Cherisse confirmed their agreement with an uncertain grip.

Before she fell asleep that night, Helen made a mental note to ask Pudge to dig out the old hatbox from the back of her bedroom closet. She knew she'd stashed away some of the corniest material she'd ever written and wanted Cherisse to see it. For the first time since her accident she slept through the night without a painkiller.

As days unfolded into weeks, Helen felt she was taking one step forward and two steps back. First, she had to adjust to having someone with her each minute of every hour. Fortunately, Pudge was able to tackle tasks he could do upstairs or in the attic when Jolly Jake arrived to dole out his daily dose of cruelty. Late in the afternoon, Doris often stopped to drop off supper and to leave Cherisse so she could eat and chat with Helen. Then either Kristi or Jenna came to spend the night.

Helen was intrigued with funky but gentle Jenna, who always provided aid when asked. Kristi, on the other hand, was an expert caregiver but could be stern and abrupt. She'd had words with Kristi their second night together, when Helen whimpered it was too painful to get up and go to the bathroom.

"Bring me the bedpan," she begged. "Just this once. It's too hard to pull up my pajama bottoms."

"Not on your life," Kristi retorted. "You've gotta move your butt or you'll never be able to do anything."

Helen almost sent her packing right on the spot. Instead, she swallowed her pride, coped with her pain, and made her trip to the bathroom. When she returned to her bed, Kristi had plumped her pillows and given her a warm smile.

After that incident, she was glad she'd complied with Kristi's order. The two developed an easy friendship, and Helen enjoyed the family tales Kristi told. She knew she was in for a treat when Kristi ran her hand through her auburn bangs and lifted her chin as an introduction to the story she was about to share.

"That Simpkins bunch is so different from my family." Kristi fluffed a pillow on the couch and nestled in. "At my house, we always looked out for ourselves. My sister and me—we always made sure one of us didn't do more work than the other."

Helen chuckled. "Sounds like Haley and me."

"Our mom and dad were the same—always squabbling over whose turn it was to do this and do that." Kristi shuddered at the memory. "But Pudge's family? When one falls down, another one picks him up. When one's sick, another one helps out. Sometimes I think they're like a pack of gypsies. Always doing stuff together. But you know what? It sure works!"

Helen nodded. "They all pitched in when their mother died."

Kristi grew somber. "That about killed every one of them. That little bitty woman was a tower of strength for her kids. Taught 'em how to work and raised 'em not to have a selfish bone in their bodies."

Kristi went on at great length about how she wished Jenna could be more like that. "She's so independent—wants everything her own way. I'm scared to death she's going to break up with Noah. That's her boyfriend, Noah. The thing of it is . . ." she stopped to consider her words. "He's a real good fit with our family. But I'm beginning to wonder if we all like him better'n Jenna does."

When she heard Jenna's version of the boyfriend saga a few evenings later, Helen knew she'd better remain neutral.

"I love it when you tell me about New York," Jenna admitted. "I hope I can live in a city someday." Her spiky dark red hair shone almost black in the lamplight. She went on to say that Noah didn't want to go anywhere much farther than Danville. "But I want to see mountains. And oceans.

And where Grandma Simpkins lived when she was growing up. All sorts of places before I die. I'm not sure . . ."

Helen let Jenna ramble on about her uncertainties before she suggested they split the slab of Doris's chocolate cake. She felt too inadequate to offer advice to Pudge's wife or his daughter on any issue.

One thing she did feel confident about was her work. Although she was frustrated with her ability to master her laptop, Helen felt happiest when she was editing. Against the background of country music and the sounds of Pudge's labor that filtered from upstairs, she used her right hand and one finger from her left to attack the files of proofs that piled up in her email in-box. Little by little, she took responsibility for getting herself to the bathroom and the kitchen table for meals. She was grateful for the attachment on her walker that enabled her to move around without putting pressure on the broken bones of her left arm.

She looked forward to supper sessions with Cherisse. She couldn't remember the last time she'd had the opportunity to step inside the scary world of a young teen and found she enjoyed Cherisse's accounts of the best ways to deal with insecurities and subtle bullying.

"Mostly, I write about it in my journal," Cherisse confided. "I'm sure Matka knows but never tries to read any of my private stuff. She's really cool that way."

"That's where you and I are both alike and different. Very different." Helen stopped to appreciate the home-cooked flavor of the hot beef sandwich Doris sent.

"How do you mean—different?" Cherisse asked with her mouth full.

"I used to write about things I hated at school to get them off my chest." Helen paused as she recalled evenings when her parents thought she was doing homework. "But my mother searched my room and read my journal. Once she slipped and referred to something I'd written, and I realized what she'd been doing."

"That's awful." Cherisse carried their plates to the sink. "What'd you do?"

"I hid my notebook almost in plain sight. I stuck it in a stack of old magazines my mother kept in our den but never looked at." Helen smiled. "And you know what? She never found it."

Cherisse's snicker showed her approval.

Helen felt these comfortable chats with Cherisse were almost worth the physical pain she was enduring. She also found herself getting sucked into the evolving soap opera between Jenna and Noah.

"I wish if they're going to break up, they'd get on with it," Kristi admitted one evening. "Pudge oughtta tell both of 'em that, but he won't get involved. I think he wants to have Noah for a son-in-law."

Helen couldn't bring herself to tell Kristi she didn't blame Jenna for feeling restless. Instead, Helen opted to stay neutral. She'd always thought that wading into the middle of family disputes was like walking through a minefield. She guessed some things never changed.

At the end of four weeks, her routine had become the new normal. She still recoiled at Jake's impossible demands but rejoiced when she saw the bulging anniversary issue of *The Arch* would meet its deadline. She was grateful she'd been able to work on her laptop, albeit awkwardly, more than a thousand miles from her office.

With only two weeks to go in her recovery, she could hardly wait for her appointment with Dr. Patel. Pudge asked a buddy if he could borrow a specially-equipped van to help transport Helen to the doctor's office.

When the March day for her appointment dawned raw and blustery, she was grateful that Pudge had thought to get the van and take the wheelchair. She would have had trouble navigating her walker into the wind but was eager to demonstrate to her surgeon how nimble she was with it indoors.

"How's my beautiful patient today?" Dr. Patel greeted her warmly. She found his canned question didn't annoy her this time. After all, she could feel the vibrant pulse of Manhattan beckoning.

He checked her latest x-rays and nodded.

"All is going well. I am pleased with your progress." He stroked his chin. "Now, tell me again what you will be doing when you resume your normal life."

She could feel the excitement mounting as she spoke of her job and its intellectual challenges.

"Your office. It is near where you live in the Village, right?" He studied her thoughtfully.

"Actually, our publishing hub is in Midtown," she explained.

"So you drive? Take a taxi?"

She laughed. "Oh, no, I don't keep a car in the city. And a cab is too expensive." She began to falter. "I—I ride the subway."

Watching as he continued to rub his chin and study her, she squirmed.

"That part I do not like." He spoke softly. "I want you totally well, absolutely healed before you subject yourself to crowds of people. They push and they shove. You know what I mean."

"But that's my life. I've dealt with it for years." She tried to remain calm but could feel the panic rising.

"My beautiful patient, I do not want you broken again. You understand?" He spoke quietly but forcefully. "When you return to New York after twelve weeks of healing, you will be strong. Good as new."

"Twelve? Twelve weeks?" She grasped the chair arms to keep from sliding to the floor. "That's—that will be in May!"

"It's for the best. And you have good help here." He rose as she began to feel herself crumbling. "I will see you in four more weeks."

Pudge

He couldn't believe Helen was the same person he'd driven to her appointment. She had been ready to conquer the world. But the one he was driving home was a shrunken, sniveling mess.

He never knew what to do with females who burst into tears. Probably 'cause he'd never seen his mom fall apart, he decided. And when his wife or daughter went to pieces, he always seemed to come up with the wrong words. Now it was the same with Helen.

"It's not the end of the world." When he tried to reassure her, she sobbed harder. He forced her wheelchair into the wind, up the ramp, and into her house.

"Jiminy, Helen, the doc's just looking out for your own good." He helped her out of her coat and into bed, then stood bewildered as she turned away and pulled the covers over her head.

"You go ahead and have yourself a good cry. I'm gonna go upstairs and work for awhile." As he left the room he complained, "One of us might as well get something done."

If Helen's recovery was inching along at a snail's pace, Pudge felt his work on the house was taking even longer. "I'm afraid she's gonna think I'm padding my hours," he confessed to Kristi as they shared a pizza with Jenna. "I thought I'd have this job wrapped up in three or four weeks, but I honestly think it could take a year if I let it. Sometimes I bring down a box stuffed with junk from the attic, and Helen wants to tell me about every single thing in it. That really slows me down."

He reached for another slice. "Funny thing though. I do think sorting through some of that mess helped her get a grip after she found out she can't go home till May. I wish I could do more."

"Oh, Pudge, you're such a pushover." Kristi split the last slice and shared it with Jenna. "Sometimes you've gotta give her—what do they call it—tough love. Don't pamper her."

"That may be easy for you to say, but me? I couldn't never be mean to Helen. Even if it's good for her." He flattened the pizza box and placed it in with the recycling. "Here. I'm in charge of dessert." He dropped a bag of Nutter Butter cookies in the middle of the table.

"I like talking with her after the ten o'clock news." Jenna devoured a cookie with two bites. "Sometimes, when she tells me about New York, I almost feel like I've been there. And when I say something, <u>she</u> always listens."

Pudge saw Jenna shoot a straight look in her mother's direction and wondered what that was about. Oh well, he thought, with women you never knew.

"She talks with me before we go to bed too." Kristi broke the silence. "And you're right, Jenna," she added, "she listens. Always."

Pudge

April

Pudge was glad to see that once Helen knew she had to stay put till May, she seemed to make up her mind to get interested in the work on the house.

"If I'm going to be selling this place," she told him one day late in March, "I should get rid of every single thing I don't want. And that includes those cartons of ridiculous costumes Haley wore when she twirled. Lord Almighty!"

"All of 'em?" He'd better make sure. "There must be five or six great big boxes."

"Every one of them."

He turned so she couldn't see him smile. He could tell by her tone that she was getting a real kick out of throwing away her sister's sparkly brittle dresses that had been stored in the attic for years.

After Helen watched him toss those boxes into a load of trash on his truck, she began to move like she had some purpose. She could really get around on that walker of hers and had decided which things could go straight to the dump. By mid-April, when he thought he could wrap up his work in a day or two, she hit him with another assignment.

"I've heard you say you painted and papered for Doris," she said as they shared some darn good soup she'd made. He watched dust mites dance in the rays of spring sunshine that poured through the long windows and wondered what she had in mind now.

"If you're not in a huge hurry, it'd be great if you could put up fresh paper and do some painting all over the house."

He dunked a saltine in his soup. "I could do that," he agreed. "Nobody's beatin' down my door to ask me to come to work." He thought for a moment. "But you know hardly anybody's putting up wallpaper anymore."

"I know, but I'm thinking of textured paper. No patterns." She passed the bowl of crackers to him. "Why don't you bring me some color charts and wallpaper books from the hardware store? I'm ready to make this house look as if it belongs in the twenty-first century."

For the next few weeks, he felt he could barely keep up with himself. For one thing, Helen never took a nap anymore. He could see what a force she must be in her New York office when she made up her mind to tackle something big. Even Kristi and Jenna got into the spirit of Helen's updating project.

"I know it's kinda old-fashioned, but I think a pale blue paper with tiny flowers would look nice in that front bedroom," Kristi said one evening at supper. "With white curtains. I always wanted a room like that when I was growing up."

"You'll have trouble talking Helen into that." Jenna bit

into a sloppy joe. "She's more of a bright-color person if you ask me."

"We'll see."

Pudge knew he didn't want to be anywhere near the Hamilton house when his wife and daughter offered their suggestions to Helen. He decided right then and there to be at home watching American Pickers that night.

Helen

She'd never realized her parents' house had such potential for coming alive. She almost cheered when she saw her mother's heavy brocade draperies hit the floor in a dusty heap and welcomed the light the new window treatment allowed. She marveled at Pudge's stamina as he hauled out endless boxes of her dad's crumbling financial papers and armloads of her mom's dressy clothes that the historical society might want.

Each evening she looked forward to a call from Burt, who painted grim pictures of Manhattan emerging from a fierce winter; she knew he was only trying to make her feel better about having to stay in Rockwell. When he shared a tale about Miss Adelaide's latest caper with a stack of sticky notes, she snickered then realized with a pang that he might have a hard time relinquishing her cat when she returned.

She enjoyed her growing friendship with Kristi and Jenna and began to admire their mother-daughter relationship. No two women were more dissimilar, she thought. Kristi was forthright and totally traditional, whereas Jenna was funky and full of dreams. Still, in spite of their differences, they shared boundless love and appreciation for each other.

One late afternoon, however, when Cherisse bounced in with one of Doris's chicken pot pies, Helen realized that it was the mealtimes with this budding teen that she relished most.

"There's little green things poking through that dirt in the front yard." Cherisse deposited the heavy bag of food on the kitchen table. "And guess what: Miss Taylor loved the theme I wrote on making a Polish dinner. Said it made her hungry."

Helen's appetite surged at Cherisse's news. Although she'd read the essay and made a couple of suggestions, she'd been impressed with this youngster's ability to appeal to a reader's senses.

"That's great!

"Couldn't have done it without you."

They sat at Helen's kitchen table and discussed the fun of finding the right word and placing it where it would have the best effect. The pot pie, with its creamy gravy and Doris's own flaky crust, disappeared as they talked.

Afterward, Cherisse grew quiet before she spoke.

"I need to ask you something. But you don't have to say yes if you don't want to." She focused on folding her paper napkin into a tiny fan.

"Sure!" Helen tried to sound upbeat but was concerned. Cherisse had become uneasy.

"Remember how we talked about not having friends at school? You know, you said you had trouble with that like I do." Cherisse continued to refold her napkin. "A few days ago I started talking to this girl who just moved here. Her name's Ruby and she's—she's real shy."

Helen remained quiet.

"I kinda told her about you and the house you live in. She's not real interested in English, but she loves antiques. So I wondered—"

"If you could introduce her to <u>me</u>?" Helen chuckled. "Some kids would classify me as an antique."

"Oh, no!" Cherisse's face reddened. "I didn't mean—"

"Sorry." Helen patted her arm. "I couldn't resist."

"I thought—well, I wondered if I could bring her over here sometime—to meet you and see some of the stuff you have. I think Ruby'd love it."

"You bring her any time." Helen felt flattered. This place could use a few more young people, she thought. "The sooner, the better. I do hope to go back to New York next month."

"Thanks! Thanks a lot." When Cherisse engulfed her with a heartfelt hug, Helen felt a warm glow spread through her.

"Let's go back to the living room till Doris comes to pick you up," she suggested. "You can tell me more about Ruby." It was then she realized she was missing something.

"Cherisse!" she exclaimed. "I don't have my walker with me. I bet I left it in the living room."

In an instant Cherisse popped out of her chair and ran out of the kitchen.

"It's right by your chair," she called. "Want me to bring it to you?"

Helen grinned. "No, that's okay. If I made it to the kitchen, I can make it back." Hobbling to the living room, she spotted her walker and gave Cherisse a high-five.

"Things are starting to look up, kiddo," she said. "For both of us."

Monty

June

He hated to admit it, but he kind of missed Al on this trip to Danville. He'd learned to tolerate the guy's terrible jokes and grown to look forward to his company. But Al had called on Monday to say he'd jumped at the chance to take an opening for a surgical procedure he needed. He didn't elaborate but did add he ought to be able to golf by August.

On hearing that news, Gordon Strunke insisted that Monty make today's journey alone. Al and Monty had ruled out the locations in Nebraska, Indiana, and Tennessee for various reasons and had narrowed their recommendation for the new site to Janesville and Danville.

"Go see for yourself. Right now." Strunke twisted his left ear lobe as he did when he was passionate about a topic. "The Board is getting antsy. Make sure you check out available labor force."

Monty also hated to admit he could have used a dose of Al's upbeat, laid-back attitude. Since Sunday when he dropped off Theo at basketball camp, Monty had felt limp and drained. Worse yet, he couldn't identify the cause.

He'd thought his joy would bubble over when he placed Theo in such a promising athletic environment, but he felt like a has-been when he saw the photo of his own team near the back of the trophy room. He and his buddies had been ecstatic that year when they edged Ohio State, but the yellowing picture punched him in the gut.

The day he delivered Theo to camp had been awkward from the get-go. A cloud of deadly silence filled the car from the time he and Theo left home until they reached Evanston. Monty's attempts to make animated conversation were blocked with abrupt yes and no answers. The chill in the air was so noticeable he felt like he could turn off the air conditioner. When he left Theo with his roommate Sam, a strapping country boy with bulging muscles and a firm grip, he tried to give his son a hug. But Theo shrugged and turned away.

He sighed as he turned off the highway and onto Rockwell's Main Street. At least he'd be uplifted by the bustling crowd in The Boulder while he ate the best French toast in the world. However, when he opened the door to the familiar décor and welcoming aromas, he was startled by the inactivity.

A handful of people chatted in a few booths, while one table was occupied by an elderly man doing a crossword puzzle. The pony-tailed server, who usually dashed from customer to customer, rolled silverware in napkins at a table near the back.

Monty scoped out the dining area and opted for a stool at the counter next to the red-haired fellow he remembered seeing a few months ago.

"Pretty quiet today." He hoped the guy wouldn't take offense at his observation.

"Today and every day." The response was flat. "Hey, Tiffany. You got a live one here."

"French toast, right?" Tiffany smiled. "And coffee. With a little cream."

"I don't know how you remember. I've only been here two or three times."

"A knack I picked up from my grandma." She poured steaming coffee into his cup and set two creamers in front of him.

"Is she here?" he wondered.

"Not yet."

"Hope she's okay." He hated to think the self-possessed lady with the cane—Tommy Panczyk's sister—might be ill.

"Yes and no."

God, he thought as the girl gazed steadily at him, her gray eyes are just like her grandmother's.

"I mean, she's not sick sick, if you know what I mean. But it's hard for her to see the place so empty."

"Hard on all of us," the fellow next to him added.

Monty stuck out his hand. "Monty Cooper."

"Pudge Simpkins."

The fingers that grasped Monty's felt strong and calloused. A sincere grin revealed a gap between his front teeth, and his cowlick looked like Opie's on the old Andy Griffith Show.

"I can tell you're not from around here." Monty felt Pudge's sweeping evaluation of his navy blazer and crisp white shirt. "So you prob'ly don't know we've had a real kick in the butt."

"Like?" Monty sipped his rich coffee and waited for an explanation.

"Like our biggest employer shut down and left the whole dern town out on a shaky limb." Pudge stuffed a wedge of cinnamon roll into his mouth.

"God. How awful." At a loss for words, Monty shook his head and waited for Pudge to continue. But the guy methodically destroyed his cinnamon roll in silence. At last Monty was relieved when Tiffany delivered his platter of French toast.

"This has to be really tough on Mrs. Lochschmidt," he observed, recalling her account of how hard she and her sister had worked to get The Boulder established.

"Dern near killing her." Pudge ran his fork around his plate to corral the last crumbs of his roll. "Seems to get worse every week. Folks can't afford to eat out since Midwest shut down." He swiveled on his stool. "Me? I'm doing odd jobs right now but try to stop in every day."

Searching for words, Monty let his gaze sweep the room. "Last time I was in, she showed me all the old pictures on her wall. This place has quite a history."

"Yep—and all because of Miss D."

Monty raised his eyebrows but didn't ask.

"We're talking about the same old gal—just calling her different names." Pudge sipped his cream soda. "You shoulda seen her in action when my mom died a few months ago. Cooked a big dinner and brought it over to the Baptist Church. Must've served close to three hundred.

"Oh, yeah, her whole family here pitched in," Pudge added. "But her and my mom went to school together—kids from the wrong side of the tracks who stuck up for each other. She wasn't about to let friends and family say good-bye to my mom without a decent meal."

Monty was so absorbed with the scene Pudge described that he was startled by his next question.

"So what brings you to Rockwell? Not much going on here right now." Pudge slid from his stool and picked up his bill.

"On my way to Danville." Suddenly, Monty felt embarrassed by his natty attire. "Business-related work. But I'd eaten here before—"

"Not much going on there either," Pudge interrupted. "Just a lot more of it." He nodded and headed toward the cash register. "Maybe I'll see you again sometime."

"Hope so." Monty watched Pudge amble out the door and climb into the old pickup in the parking lot. Here was a fellow who'd hit rock bottom and possibly didn't know it. But he did seem to have a lot of common sense. And Pudge's unsolicited opinion of Danville made Monty wonder if he should scrutinize that location more closely. Maybe he and Al would be recommending Janesville after all.

That Pudge guy knew what he was talking about, he thought as he made his way home on the interstate. After taking the time to explore more of Danville, Monty had been surprised by all the vacant storefronts downtown. He talked with a few discouraged people at a convenience store and was shocked by the number of homes for sale. Next week, as soon as Al was able, the two of them would travel up to Janesville.

Later that day, however, Monty found himself jolted from his iron-clad routine. He'd used the first few minutes after he arrived home from Danville to check his messages and learned to his satisfaction that his Chamber lunch and Community Pantry meeting were scheduled in their proper time slots the next day. Content, he knew he couldn't squeeze much more out of his well-ordered life.

On his way to the fridge, he heard Claire answer the phone. Her lengthy silence as she listened was shattered by a scream he would never forget. Rushing to her side, he grabbed the phone and heard the words from the basketball camp director: Theo had not shown up for the evening meal, and when his roommate returned to the dorm, he found Theo unresponsive in his bed with a note and an empty bottle of pills on the nightstand. He'd been taken to Evanston Hospital, where his stomach was pumped. Doctors felt he would recover but advised Monty and his wife to come as soon as possible.

Clutching the steering wheel with clammy hands, Monty cursed the day that officials decided not to put a more complete interstate link from the western suburbs to the northern ones. He felt the welcome surge of power as he floored the accelerator and sped across I-88 and the Tri-State. But when he turned onto Dempster to thread his way through local streets and roads, he felt he had come to a standstill. The speedometer read sixty.

"Dammit!" He pounded the wheel in frustration.

Claire whimpered and chewed her nails, while the only sounds from the backseat were Cassidy's occasional sniffles.

From the moment they pushed through the revolving door and allowed themselves to be swallowed by the hospital, Monty felt all control slipping away. An efficient matron at the front desk reported that Theo had been moved from the ER into a room where he was being treated.

They stared numbly at each other as the elevator rose, then deposited them on Theo's floor. A nurse suggested they make themselves comfortable in a small waiting room while she checked on Theo. When she returned, Monty could tell by her bright smile that this situation was going to be tough. She suggested that they visit with Theo briefly, one at a time. Monty opted to let Claire go first.

While Cassidy thumbed through an old issue of *People,* Monty studied the tile floor and wondered how they'd arrived at this point in their lives. Hours seemed to pass before Claire reappeared, pale and tearful, yet when he looked at the clock on the wall, he realized she'd been with Theo for six minutes.

"Your turn," Claire croaked. "He's not awake." Monty took a deep breath and forced himself to take the painful steps down the sterile hall to Theo's room.

He wasn't quite prepared for the sight of his son. Tethered to tubes and monitors, Theo looked whiter than the freshly laundered sheets. So thin. So helpless. So vulnerable. Monty brushed away the mist that clouded his vision and approached the bed.

"Hey, Theo. I'm here. We—we love you." When he

covered Theo's hand with his own, he felt his son's fingers fold around his. Grateful to feel his son's life pulsing through his veins, he let the tears flow freely down his cheeks. Not once did he check his watch to see how long he stayed.

No one thought about an evening meal. Instead, they were able to learn from the resident on duty that Theo had overdosed on painkillers.

"A fairly common occurrence among teens these days." The young woman's dark eyes looked weary behind heavy glasses. "Any idea where he got them?"

"I—I have some. For—for my—my back pain." Claire's composure seemed to dwindle as she spoke. "In my—my medicine cabinet. In—in our private bathroom. But Theo never—"

"Never what?" The doctor glanced up from her notes, pen in mid-air.

"This—this morning I wondered if—if there weren't as many pills. As there should have been." Monty reached for her arm as she began to tremble. "I never thought—"

"Parents never do," the doctor said kindly but firmly. "But don't blame yourself. We need to know what triggered his desperation. In the meantime, it's best for everyone if you go home and get some rest. We'll take care of Theo and you need to look after yourselves."

Unhinged by the scene at the hospital, Monty felt like a robot as he began the drive back to Naperville. Claire sat in a self-imposed shell of silence, while Cass gasped out fragments of phrases and tried to hold back tears.

"Theo's been different lately."

"What do you mean—different?" Dammit, he thought as

he crawled through the streets and roads leading back to the Tri-State, then wondered what the hurry was. No one was home anyway.

"I dunno. Quiet, I guess." Cass blew her nose. "Never teases me anymore. Just shuts himself in his room and turns on that classical music." She spent their entire time on the Tri-State sobbing. Claire sat still as a statue.

As he zipped along the expressway, Monty tried to process Cass's take on things. She was right: Theo had become withdrawn in the last few weeks—something Monty had attributed to adolescent moodiness. He'd always thought he and Theo had been pretty good buddies in the time slots he reserved for his son. In fact, he always believed he'd been an exemplary dad to both of his kids, serving on committees that benefited their activities. A lot of guys never did any of that.

When they arrived home, Cass took out the peanut butter jar.

"Sandwich, Dad?"

"Sure. Thanks." He noticed Claire had already poured herself a glass of wine and given him a look that stated she did not want to talk. At least not then.

In the morning, he felt drugged. He wished they'd stayed at the hospital, but the doctor had insisted the three of them needed their rest. What rest? Hell, he grunted, he must have dozed off for only a few minutes several times during the night, while Claire had tossed from the moment she put her head on the pillow.

Groggily they retraced their route to Evanston while Cass went to soccer practice. When they checked on Theo, they found he was with a chaplain, so they opted to pick up his belongings at the dorm and visit him later.

When Monty spotted clusters of guys laughing together as they returned from basketball clinic, he felt a cloud of sadness engulf him. Theo should be out there too, having the time of his life. But their wan and listless son now lay limp on a hospital bed, waiting to be evaluated.

Wordlessly, Claire emptied Theo's dresser and placed his clothes in the bag he'd brought to camp. When she picked up his basketball shoes, Monty thought he might lose it. He remembered how much fun he had the day he and Theo bought those fancy shoes. Now he wondered how long Theo had faked the part of the eager athlete.

"Shit!" one of the group of teens exclaimed when he saw adults in the room.

Offering Monty a firm handshake, Sam switched his demeanor from rowdy to subdued.

"Uh, we gotta go," another mumbled as he headed out the door.

"Sorry." The first student gave a half-hearted wave as he made his escape from the awkward situation.

"We came to pick up Theo's things." Claire's words sounded wooden as she tenderly placed their son's clothes in the bag he'd brought to camp.

Sam motioned for Monty to sit in the desk chair, then stuffed his hands in his pockets and looked out the window.

"Theo's a great guy." He paused and took a deep breath. "But I could see something's been bugging him."

Monty marveled at the perception of this kid who'd just met his son. "Tell us. Please," he urged. "Good. Bad. We need to hear it."

Claire perched on the side of the bed and stopped packing. Monty felt his mouth go dry as Sam recounted the first three days of camp. Everything had gone okay till a coach yelled at Theo for dribbling the ball too high and for being so skinny.

"I felt sorry for him," Sam said. "The coach told him he'd have to beef up if he wanted to play ball. Bullied him right there in front of everybody." He sighed. "I think Theo left practice early—and he sure didn't want to talk about it that night."

"Dammit." Old emotions Monty hadn't dealt with in years stirred inside him. "Sounds like a couple of Big Ten coaches I used to play against."

"Thank you, Sam." Claire zipped Theo's bag. "At least now we know what's bothering him." She stood, ready to leave. "C'mon, Monty. Let's go see our boy."

They were walking out of the room when Sam stammered, "If—if I hadn't forgotten my—my meal pass, I wouldn't have come back—back to the dorm and . . ."

Seeing Sam's ashen face, Monty realized how close they had come to losing Theo.

"God, Sam, it was a miracle," were the only words Monty could choke out. When he saw Claire wobble, he took her arm and steered her outside into the fresh air and toward the car.

During the next week, Monty took a few days of sick leave so he and Claire could spend time with Theo as they tried to re-connect. The afternoon before he was to be dismissed they endured a lengthy session with a counselor who told them their son was "a great kid who needs to accept himself as he is."

Puzzled, Monty asked, "You mean he thinks he's too skinny to be a good ball player? We can help beef him up."

He knew he'd never forget the shock on the counselor's face as he gazed at them. "You really don't know, do you."

"Don't know what?" Monty felt his face reddening as he shouted, "For God's sake, spit it out!"

"Your kid is miserable."

Monty knew the guy was way off base. "That's crap and you know it. Theo has everything."

"Everything," the counselor delivered his message gently, "but the courage to tell you he's gay. He's known for awhile but is terrified to tell you."

Each word hit Monty like an iron bar across his face. Desperately he tried to respond. Finally, he blurted, "Not my kid. Not Theo!"

"Maybe we all can work on that together when he feels better." The counselor rose. "I think we've done enough for now."

Monty stumbled along behind Claire, who strode to the car, keys in her hand. He hardly remembered the ride home, only the blur of the suburban sprawl as he stared through the window.

That night, as they huddled together in bed, Claire admitted she'd wondered about Theo. Monty responded that he'd never considered their son's sexual preference and thought the counselor was way off base.

"We'll have to let Theo tell us," Claire said sleepily. "I think we'll be okay."

But Monty was chilled by the thought and wondered if he might have to run to the bathroom and puke. All night long, when sleep was ready to descend, he'd recall a moment from Theo's childhood when they cheered together at the Bulls games that Monty had carefully carved into his calendar. He'd never taken him to any sissy theatrical productions. And sure as hell not ballet. Not his son! God, he thought, that counselor's gotta be wrong. When he wakened and realized he'd slept only ninety minutes, he wished he'd been smart enough to take a few more sick days.

He struggled that morning as he went through the motions of his regular chores at work. His mind wandered during a high-level strategic company planning session where he was again urged to produce a recommendation for an expansion facility. Opting to eat lunch at his desk, he rubbed his head as he sought to find vague new excuses for missing his usual civic meetings for the next month. He realized he had no interest in any of them. Not now.

Still, he knew all of his associates had heard about Theo's problems. Everyone was so damn nice to him, he fretted. However, if he hated wallowing in the kindness of his social acquaintances, he loathed even more the wall of silence he met in his own house.

Theo hardly spoke during his first days home from the hospital but built an impenetrable cocoon around himself the week he'd dreamed of dancing in Aspen. Claire was brutally chipper as she prepared Theo's favorite meatballs not once but twice that week. As Monty picked at his food he realized Cassidy was scrutinizing her brother. Theo ate his meals without a word, then went to his room. God, Monty fumed, would his family ever talk to each other again!

Claire assumed the job of driving Theo to his counseling sessions each week—one with an individual therapist and the other with a group—but rarely commented on her time with their son. Instead, she ranted about the scorching dry spell that withered her flowers.

After a break in the heat wave, she and Monty fell into the habit of sitting silently on their patio after dinner, listening to the drone of crickets and the low hum of conversation between Theo and Cass that wafted from his bedroom window.

"Monty, you need to get some new Dockers," she told him one evening as she followed him into the house. "Those are starting to droop."

"Yep." It was easier to agree than to admit that he had no appetite and was sick with guilt over having manipulated Theo into going to that basketball camp. In his heart, he knew he'd been the source of many of his son's problems, but he had no idea how to broach the subject or with whom.

One evening after Theo had gone to his room, Cassidy shattered their silence.

"You guys don't get it!" She planted her feet on the kitchen floor and placed her fists on her hips. "Do you realize how scared he is to go back to school?" She glared at them. "All I can say is you'd better start talking to him or we'll find ourselves back at the effing hospital some night."

With that, she stormed outside. Soon they heard the thump of the basketball on the driveway as Cass took out her anger shooting three-pointers.

Stunned, Monty looked at his wife.

Claire, pale and thoughtful, commented, "She's right, you know."

"What'll we say?" Unsure as a first-day kindergartner, he searched his mind for the words to connect with their son.

"We'll think of something." Seeing she was already on her way to Theo's room, Monty followed.

"Theo." He could hear the decisiveness in her voice. "We'd like to talk."

He wished he shared her confidence. The only emotion he could drum up was remorse.

"Sure," their son replied. "Come on in."

God, he was grateful that Claire took the lead that night. Tenderly she asked Theo the questions they'd been afraid to discuss and wondered aloud if he thought it would help to undergo counseling as a family. When Theo replied that he'd like for all of them to talk things over with Len Vogel, his therapist, they jumped on the opportunity.

"I'll check with him tomorrow," Claire promised.

Monty wished he felt more optimistic about their meeting. After all, he usually called most of the shots for their family. With this crisis, it seemed like he was chasing a crazy rabbit and never catching up.

When Len Vogel told Claire he would see them around five on Mondays and Thursdays, Monty groaned but guessed it was okay to miss meetings with the "Y" and Community Pantry boards for awhile. Suspecting a wimpy academic, he was surprised by the solid handshake he received from this

Vogel character who resembled Mike Ditka at the peak of his career.

Through the next few weeks all thoughts of civic meetings slipped from his mind as Monty became acquainted with this stranger named Theo who lived under his roof. Vogel assured Monty and Claire that their son was "the same Theo you've always loved but just going down a little different path from the one you chose for him." Monty liked that. He could live with that. What he could not live with was Theo gone forever from their lives.

Monty

August—September

For the first time, he began to see the world through Theo's eyes and to understand his son's dread of returning to his old school. When Vogel suggested they look at Chicago Academy as an alternative, Monty and Claire discussed it with Theo and were stunned at his enthusiastic reaction to the possibility of attending a school that offered a dance curriculum.

The Wednesday before Labor Day, when Monty had planned one last trip to Danville the following day, he asked Theo if he'd like to ride along.

"I could use some good company. Plus, I want to take you to the little restaurant that serves the world's best French toast. You up for that?"

"Sure. You buying?" Theo's eyes sparkled with anticipation. Monty knew if he'd asked this kid the same question last spring, he'd have shrugged and said, "Whatever." Could it be that his son, now they were beginning to know each other better, might actually want to spend some time with his old dad?

As they followed the ribbon of ragged state highway that wove its way between endless fields of withering corn and yellowing soybeans, Theo asked, "Why do you think people choose to live out here?"

"I wondered that myself. Then I remembered my own hometown and all the fun we could drum up." Monty was quiet for a moment as he recalled his pals. "One of my friends had a rusty old Plymouth that drove like a tank. We'd pool our change to buy gas and take that thing into Moline. Thought life didn't get any better than that."

Monty slowed to make the turn into Rockwell. "I guess people just choose to live where it feels like home."

Theo studied the string of neglected houses that lined the main street, then pointed to a large rambling building.

"What's that?"

"Used to be the industrial hub here. Midwest Manufacturing, I believe." He pulled up at the curb across the street and stared at the deserted building. "Their corporate headquarters merged operations and closed the plant."

"Musta hurt a lot of people."

"Yep." Monty edged the Beemer back onto the bumpy brick street and drove a few blocks. "Well, there she sits," he announced. "Let's go find some French toast."

"The Boulder? Why'd they name it for a rock?" Surveying the modest white cement-block building with its royal blue trim, Theo stretched as he climbed from the car.

"It's the name of their high-school team. The Boulders. You know, from <u>Rock</u>well." When Monty saw the tolerant look Theo shot him, he added, "Don't judge it. Just enjoy the food. The owner is a good old soul. And her brother was Tommy Panczyk. You've heard his piano music."

"No shit!" Theo lengthened his stride as he approached the restaurant.

"She's always been nice to me," Monty explained, "and she's gone through some lean times since Midwest closed. I figured we could give her some business and have a good breakfast ourselves."

When he opened the door, he took a deep breath of the familiar fragrances of home cooking but was disheartened to find only a handful of customers. Still, there was a hum of steady activity with crews of helpers setting up a few extra tables. As he and Theo headed toward a booth, one of the workers bumped into Monty.

"Sorry." The red-haired guy apologized and shifted the folding chairs he was carrying. "Hey," he said, "we met before. At the counter a while back. Remember?" He stuck out his hand.

"Uh. Yeah." Monty dug deep into his memory. "Pudge, right? Good to see you again." He felt the sand-papery texture of the guy's palm against his. "Monty. Monty Cooper. And my son, Theo. What's going on here?"

"Comfort Food Day. Miss D'll wanta see you. I'll go get her so she can tell you all about it."

Sliding across the blue vinyl booth, Theo rolled his eyes as a server approached.

"Hi, Mr. Cooper." She swished her ponytail and asked if they wanted French toast.

"You never forget, do you Tiffany? Plus coffee for me and a large orange juice for my son."

After she'd left for the kitchen, he explained. "Her grandma's Mrs. Lochschmidt, the one who owns this place. Tiffany's mom, Darcy, manages it."

"Dad! How do you know all this shit?"

God, Monty thought, he hoped his son wasn't going to climb on his high horse and think they were slumming. He was ready to spit out a sarcastic reply when the rhythmic sound of a cane on the tile floor stopped him.

"I heard you was here. Haven't seen you in a coon's age." He stood to greet this woman he'd grown to appreciate and carefully enfolded her gnarled hand in his.

"Can you join us for a minute? I want you to meet my son, Theo." He motioned for her to sit beside him.

"Theo, is it? Good Polish name. My grandpa's, in fact. I like that." Theo blushed under her genuine warmth.

"You been sick?" she asked. Monty stiffened when she turned her attention on him. "You're lookin' a little puny."

"Had a virus a few weeks ago." He could tell by the way she inspected him she knew he was lying. "Pudge said you'd tell us about what's going on here today."

"Well," she motioned for Tiffany to bring her a cup of coffee, then settled into her story. Between sips, she explained how she and Darcy came up with an idea to boost the morale of the folks in Rockwell. One evening after closing, they talked about how happy everyone had been at the funeral dinner for Pudge's mom and wished they could do something to make them feel good again. Together, they hatched the idea of "Comfort Food Day." Every person in town who wanted to eat would come and pay whatever they could on a certain day once a month. From four-thirty to seven, she

163

added. Folks out of work might drop a quarter in the basket that Cherisse passed, but those who were better off were encouraged to pay what they thought the supper was worth. She and Darcy doubted they'd come close to breaking even but decided they had to do it.

"Last month was our first time," she said. "And would you believe we cleared eight dollars and seventy-five cents."

"Incredible." Monty thought they would have lost a bundle. "How'd you manage that?"

Her eyes sparkled. "Someone gave us a hundred-dollar bill. And there were several twenties."

Theo whistled softly. "How many came?"

"Oh, eighty to ninety. We're lookin' for more tonight." She drained her cup. "And you know what? Everybody here had a great time—rich, poor, all laughin' and tellin' old stories about stuff that went on in Rockwell years ago."

"What did you serve?" Theo asked.

"Homemade chicken and noodles with mashed potatoes. Tonight it'll be Swiss steak." She sighed. "It's the least we can do for our town. These folks have supported us since the day we opened."

She leaned on the table as she rose, then focused on Theo.

"I want you to come back, young man. Somehow," she fixed her gaze on him, "you make me think of my brother Tommy. I'd like to tell you about him when I'm not so busy."

Before Theo could reply, Pudge dashed up and asked how many chairs she wanted at the tables in the back room.

"As many as you can get in." She set her jaw. "These two here are on their way to Danville. Maybe goin' to put in a new factory there, so they'll be stoppin' in from time to time, I hope."

"Good luck." Pudge flashed his grin at Monty and Theo. "Maybe some of us can get jobs there if you do."

"Glad to see you like our French toast as much as your dad does." Mrs. Lochschmidt smiled as she appraised Theo's clean plate. "And I'm serious." she called over her shoulder as she hobbled toward the kitchen. "You come back and I'll tell you more about my brother."

As he paid his bill, Monty fought back the lump in his throat. Not only was Mrs. Lochschmidt a great lady and a superb cook, but she had amazing perception. When she met Theo, she realized he might be fighting some of the battles her brother had when he was growing up as a talented gay teen in a small town. She wanted to assure Theo, in some way, that he was going to be just fine.

As they continued on their way to Danville, however, Monty wished that Al were riding with him instead of Theo. Al would've gazed out the window, made cracks about the flat landscape, and told a few lame jokes. But Theo kept pelting him with questions that made him squirm: "S'pose, Dad, we could stop at The Boulder on our way back? It'd be fun to go to that dinner they're having—what'd she call it? Swiss steak? I've never had that . . . Sounds a lot better than McDonald's . . . Why doesn't our family ever eat at restaurants like that? Everywhere we go is a franchise. Even the nice places . . . I really liked Mrs. Lochschmidt and the few people I met. Sounds like they've got each other's backs.

Not like the phony country club members at home. Why don't we know people like that? . . . That empty old factory building sure looks sad. Couldn't it be used for something?" God, Monty thought, had he ever opened a can of worms when he'd brought his son along!

In the meeting with the Danville Chamber of Commerce official that afternoon, Monty found himself still distracted by Theo's questions. He tried to force his attention on the potential Danville offered as a community but found he was more intrigued with the beads of sweat that etched a pattern down the Chamber rep's prominent forehead.

"Okay, Theo, you win," he said as they returned to their car and drove through the empty streets of Danville during what should have been rush hour. "Let's go see what this Comfort Food Day is all about."

Pudge

"**W**eren't the two of you in here this morning?" Pudge picked up a tray of rolled napkins and grinned. "Good to see you back. Especially tonight."

"After we heard about Comfort Food Day, we thought it was too good to pass up," Monty said. "You know teen-age boys. Never can fill 'em up."

"Well then, you've come to the right place." Pudge told them to join the line for the cafeteria-style meal, then find a seat. "Miss D's great-granddaughter'll walk through with a basket for donations. You can put in as little as you want." He thought for a moment. "Or as much!"

Pudge hoped they wouldn't feel out of place. He was glad Monty had left his sport coat in the car and rolled up the sleeves of his shirt. He watched while the two merged into the line, then checked the serving tubs. The mashed potatoes were running low, and the homemade applesauce would need a refill soon. He returned to the kitchen, where Darcy had everything under control.

"Where's your mom?" he asked.

"Where d'ya think? Out there somewhere talkin' with

folks. Prob'ly in the back room." Darcy lifted a large cooker of potatoes and dumped them in the tub. "She made all the apple cobblers yesterday. Guess she's earned her time off from the kitchen."

He grabbed the tub and made his way to the serving tables. Sure seemed like a load of people tonight. Tiffany had spotted Monty and his son and was directing them to the back room.

Goll-dern, he thought, Miss D really started sumthin' when she and Darcy dreamed up Comfort Food Day. Everybody in town seemed to show up, and nobody was clannish when they got here. He glanced at one table of six, where B. William Givens, the school superintendent, was engaged in a friendly animated conversation with Harvey Schmidt and Spike McGuire, who had worked with Pudge at Midwest. The three wives were laughing about who-knows-what. Any other time, Givens and his wife would be dining at the country club, while the Schmidts and McGuires scrounged up leftovers at home. It was good, he thought, as he headed into the kitchen for a big bowl of applesauce.

Pudge reminded himself to stop and talk with Harvey and Spike before they left to see if they'd turned up jobs. He'd been so busy the last couple of months that he hadn't been able to keep up with the guys from work. He'd started by organizing most of the old junk in Helen's attic and zipped through the four bedrooms upstairs much faster after she left Rockwell and returned to New York last May. Then he'd finished the painting and papering Kristi and Jenna had asked him to do. They insisted that the house had to look its best when Helen and her guy from New York came to town.

Pudge tried not to think about the big shocker that rocked his family during Labor Day weekend. Mason and his girlfriend had strolled in like they'd gone to the show or something and announced they'd gotten married. He knew they'd been living together in Danville but hadn't suspected anything like this. Poor Kristi was thrown for a loop until Mason assured her they were not pregnant. They wondered if they could rent "Grandma's house and keep it up." He guessed his mom would've liked that, but he wasn't sure his son was ready for the responsibilities that came with marriage.

Monty

"Call it a gut feeling," he told his boss two days after he and Theo returned from their trip.

Monty felt bone-deep weary from the restless nights he'd suffered as he wrestled with possible answers to Theo's casual question about a use for the empty Midwest building. Now he braced himself for Gordon Strunke's response to his startling new recommendation. His boss met his suggestion with total silence and glared at Monty before he exploded.

"Picking a location for a new plant takes a whole lot more than that, Cooper. You know that as well as I do!" Gordon Strunke growled, swiveled in his chair, and stared at the traffic on I-88 below. "Goddammit, I sent you to Danville to see how it compares to Janesville, and you come back to me with a cock-eyed idea for a different place altogether." His bushy eyebrows joined to form a dark line across his forehead.

Monty tried to counter each concern with calm professionalism. He would do nothing rash. He'd check out the demographics, study the work-force numbers, estimate the costs of converting the Midwest building into an efficient production plant, and have the data to Strunke in three weeks. In his heart he wanted his boss to experience the warmth he and Theo had found in Rockwell during Comfort Food Day. And in his heart he felt that any place capable of igniting a spark of enthusiasm in his struggling son was a place worth examining more than once.

"I've never seen you so driven, Monty," Claire observed a few days later when the two sipped a rare glass of wine in their den before dinner. Cass would be home late from a volleyball game fifty miles away, and Theo would take the ten o'clock train home after rehearsal for his school's holiday ballet.

"I know it sounds weird, but I've grown to believe in Rockwell and its people. So very much." He found it hard to explain his passion for this ordinary town to anyone—even to Claire. Especially Claire.

"But you're skipping board meetings and scrapping agendas—everything that's always been important to you."

"Yeah, well—" He ran his hand through his hair. "Guess I'm not the person I used to be."

"Me either," she admitted. "We both had a pretty tough wake-up call last summer—I'm not sure I know the 'new us.'"

"Me either," he echoed. He felt as if they were blazing a trail on fresh, uncharted ground, no longer skimming along on their former worn path to gain status.

"But I think I like the 'new us' better—whoever we are."

Startled by the intensity of the smile in her eyes, Monty realized he hadn't seen Claire expose her true emotions this openly since they started dating at Northwestern.

During the next two weeks he toiled with joyful dedication as he gathered numerical and demographic ammunition for Gordon Strunke. He assembled mountains of statistical information from local, state, and national sources but peppered his final streamlined recommendation with quotations from "Rockwell business owner" Doris Lochschmidt, and Floyd Cramer Simpkins, "work-force analyst."

"Okay, goddammit, you win." Gordon Strunke massaged his left lobe and tossed Monty's final report back on his desk the morning after he submitted it. "I stayed up past midnight reading about this Rockwell place, so I guess I'd better go have a look. You and Al work it out with Lila, and the three of us will pay this town a visit."

Monty knew the way to Lila Newberry's heart. He bribed the executive secretary with a box of Fannie May Trinidads and asked her if she could tinker with Strunke's schedule so he'd be available for the next Comfort Food Day. Although her gangly frame and poufy red hair reminded him of Carol Burnett's ditsy "Mrs.Wiggins," he admired Lila's intelligence and efficiency. He knew how closely she guarded Strunke's schedule, but he also understood the power that her famous sweet tooth held over her. After popping two pieces of candy between her boldly painted lips, Lila smiled and said she thought she could set up the requested date for Strunke.

Helen

October

Grateful that Burt was one step behind her, Helen opened the front door and waited for the lifeless air of her parents' home to overwhelm her.

"Oh, my Lord," she murmured.

Instead of walking into the usual shadowed foyer lined with heavy dust-filled draperies, she found herself embraced by the brilliant autumn rays that brought out the warmth of the pale cinnamon textured wallpaper she and Pudge had selected for the walls. Inhaling deeply, she sniffed an unfamiliar fragrance—freshly baked cookies? No way! Couldn't be.

She stopped and gazed into the adjoining living room.

"Oh, my Lord."

"I thought you said your house was—I don't know— dead or spooky or something." Burt's tone reflected the shock that Helen felt.

"I—I did." She picked up one of the sofa pillows she knew Jenna must have chosen. Sage green leaves and lilac blossoms on a creamy background tied together the new color of the walls with the faded violet of the wool carpet. "Amazing though—well, you didn't see it before—but I can't believe how freshening up the walls and adding a few pillows can bring a room to life."

"Why not? You've done a lot of that in your apartment," he reminded her as they entered the kitchen.

"But this place was a museum. Wow!" She marveled at the change made by the lemon chiffon paint she'd chosen to replace her mother's ancient wallpaper, then spotted a plate of snickerdoodles on the table. "Would you look at these? I bet Kristi baked them right here. Lord, this oven's hardly been used in years."

Burt picked up a note tucked under the cookies. "This says our supper's in the fridge. It's signed with a 'K.'"

She opened the refrigerator door and spotted three labeled plastic containers: "Sloppy joes," "fresh green beans," and "fruit." She also found a dozen eggs, milk, a small loaf of wheat bread, and a stick of butter.

"That Kristi." Helen shook her head. "She knew we'd be tired and wanted us to have something to eat."

"Pudge's wife?" he wondered. "That's somebody I need to meet—especially if she baked these." He bit into a snickerdoodle.

Munching on the soft chewy cookies, the two returned to the front hall. Helen watched Burt run his fingers over the chestnut bannister that she and Haley slid down as children. She smiled at one of the few fond childhood memories she'd managed to retain.

Burt glanced around the foyer, where the late afternoon

sun made rainbows through an oval window's beveled glass onto the worn carpet. "Reminds me of my grandma's house in New Rochelle," he said reverently.

"Reminds me too much of the house I grew up in! But now it makes me feel welcome." She wandered back into the living room where she spent so much of her recuperation time. Immediately, she sensed the presence of the people who'd helped her—Doris, with her folksy wisdom and unforgettable chicken salad sandwiches; Pudge and his family, who had emptied the house of its cluttered dreary lifelessness; and Cherisse, with whom she'd shared past and present uncertainties.

Burt waited in the doorway, allowing her to remain deep in thought. At last Helen spoke.

"I—I wish I'd had happier times in this place." The lonely feeling she had as a child washed over her. "Thanks for coming, Burt. I'm glad you're here."

"Me too." He enveloped her in one of his bear hugs. They stood in the spot her hospital bed had occupied, the area where Jolly Jake prodded her through countless hours of pain. "We'll try to have only happy times here this week. I promise."

It had been his idea to accompany her to Rockwell. At first, she pooh-poohed his suggestion, assuring him he'd be bored away from bustle of the city. But he persisted. When he reminded her the timing was perfect because he was "between cases," she waved him away. When he announced he'd always wanted to see the Midwest in the fall, she smiled and told him no. But when he looked into her eyes and admitted he really didn't want to face another week in New York by himself, she melted and agreed they'd buy two tickets to Midway instead of one. Her neighbor could look after Miss Adelaide.

Now, as they roamed the house, she was grateful to have his unsolicited appraisals.

"This might be even better than my grandma's house. I always loved to go there for Thanksgiving . . . The kitchen's great, but my favorite room's the den. It's so—I don't know—liveable . . . This place has terrific potential. Somebody's going to snap it up and make it a wonderful home for a family."

Upstairs, with Pudge's freshly painted walls stripped of their dated paper and endless photo collections of family ancestors, the bedrooms seemed spacious and inviting.

"My room," she announced, embarrassed by the blush she felt creeping across her face. As they set their carry-ons on a small bench, she realized how odd it was going to feel to have Burt beside her in the bed she'd slept in since she was twelve years old.

For a moment she thought she was dreaming. Wakened by the morning light, she sniffed the aroma of coffee and toast, stirred, then realized the other side of the bed was empty. Burt must be making breakfast. She threw on a robe, ran a brush through her hair, and hurried downstairs. Pausing in the front hall, she stopped to appreciate the new airiness that greeted her in each room. Pudge had made sure there were no more draperies, no more overpowering wallpaper, and no more clutter.

"Mornin', Sunshine." Burt turned from the stove to greet her. "Scrambled eggs and toast?"

Helen had never felt more at home in her own house. As they enjoyed their breakfast, she heard the familiar squeak of the front door.

"Anybody home?"

Burt jumped up in alarm.

"It's Pudge," she reassured him. "C'mon in."

"He's got a key?" Burt obviously had not left his New York paranoia in the city.

"Don't worry. It's okay," she whispered.

"So . . . What d'ya think?" Pudge's broad grin and stand-up cowlick were welcome sights. Realizing how much she missed this guy who'd done everything for her, she gave him a light hug.

"I can't believe it's the same place. You've been working!"

She made quick introductions as they sat down together, then told him to thank Kristi and Jenna for the food they'd left. "Especially the cookies. We could smell them when we came in."

Pudge nodded. "Kristi didn't want you to come into a house that smelled like paint and Mr. Clean."

She marveled as Burt and Pudge fell into comfortable guy-talk. Hockey? She'd known Pudge followed the Blackhawks but was shocked to learn he was up-to-date on Burt's team, the Rangers. Trucks? She'd never guessed that Burt yearned for a pickup, and that Pudge could give him buying tips. She blinked to make sure she wasn't imagining this scene where Burt and Pudge chatted in the same room like old buddies. Unbelievable!

"Got a lot of work to do upstairs but thought I'd better wait till you could tell me what you'd like done," Pudge said. "I been busy though. Doing odd jobs for Miss D's son, Doug. Remember him?"

"Do I ever! Had a big crush on him in high school," Helen admitted.

Pudge slapped his leg as he laughed, "Wait'll I tell him that."

"Don't even think it." She was dead serious. She never wanted Doug Lochschmidt to know how she'd fantasized about going to the prom with him.

"Okay, okay." Pudge brought his laughter under control. "He's doin' real good rehabbing some of them old houses on the Sweet Briar side of town. Been lucky to have the work."

He explained to Burt that he and the other Midwest workers had been scraping the bottom of the jobs barrel since the company moved its operations out of town. "It's been a year now. I'm goin' to have to find me a real job pretty soon."

"Damn corporate executives." Burt scowled. "Never give a thought to the people they hurt."

Pudge said he needed to run but wanted to remind them that Miss D's Comfort Food Day was that evening. "She's serving her special meat loaf."

When Burt suggested they might not fit in, Pudge replied that everyone fit in and it'd do them good to see that Rockwell still had some of its old spunk.

"Well—" Helen hesitated, not wanting to turn him down. "Maybe."

"Atta girl. Might even see that cute Doug Lochschmidt too." He winked and was out the door before she could think of a comeback.

Burt chortled and told her he thought they should go. After all, he reasoned, they'd never see anything like it in New York City.

As the two lingered over their third cups of coffee, she listed aloud the tasks she needed to do that day.

"Dad's first on the list. I think I'll have lunch with him." She paused. "But it might be best if you don't come this time. He'll have a hard enough time recognizing me again."

Burt replied that he'd be happy to eat the rest of Kristi's sloppy joes and make some business phone calls.

"I need to do some of that too. I want to thank Kristi for the supper and cookies. And Jenna . . . I need to catch up on her love life. And Cherisse . . .You've gotta meet her, Burt. She reminds me of myself when I was her age."

She stopped blithering and watched Burt as he stirred milk into his coffee.

"And don't forget that Comfort Food thing tonight," he added. "We need to eat somewhere."

By evening, she felt somewhat caught up with life in Rockwell. Her dad had looked puzzled when he first saw her, then smiled his wobbly grin. She'd talked with Kristi, who was worried her job might get cut and dismayed that Jenna had broken up with Noah and planned to start a nursing program in Chicago.

"Pudge isn't too happy," Kristi had told her on the phone. "He really wanted Noah for a son-in-law. But kids gotta do what kids gotta do."

Helen had sympathized with Kristi but secretly rejoiced. Now Jenna could follow her dream.

As she and Burt donned the most casual clothes they had packed, he questioned whether they needed to be at the restaurant at five o'clock.

"The only time I ever ate this early was at my grandma's." He tugged on a pair of well-cut jeans.

"Where you probably had some of the best food in your life," she reminded him.

Approaching The Boulder in their rental Nissan, she was surprised by the number of cars. The lot was full, and streets lined for a block and a half with Fords, Chevys, pickups, a couple of Cadillacs, and a BMW. When she opened the door of the familiar restaurant, she was stunned by the swell of laughter and conversation.

"Smells terrific," Burt observed.

She agreed. Pausing as they searched for seats, she saw Pudge motioning from the doorway of the back room.

"Get yourselves a tray and go through the line," he called. "I'll find you a couple of seats."

Helen basked in the soothing smells as she watched a teen-age girl fill a plate with steaming meat loaf, mashed potatoes, and green bean casserole and place it on a tray. A boy plopped a dipper full of applesauce into a small bowl and set it next to the plate.

"Rolls and butter are on the table." He smiled as he handed the food to her.

With Burt behind her, she balanced the heavy tray and made her way toward the doorway where Pudge was standing.

"Thought I told you to come early," Pudge chided as he pointed out two seats at a long table in the noisy room.

Helen grinned. The wall clock said five minutes after five.

Although she didn't recognize a soul, she knew they were all locals—except maybe the three men across from her. Judging from their rolled-up shirt sleeves and the business tone of their conversation, she knew they must be from out of town. She pegged one as either a Baptist minister or a used-car salesman with his shiny black hair and non-stop run of gab, while the second was obviously something more conservative—an accountant maybe? The third one, an uptight rising-young-executive type, seemed vaguely familiar. She knew she'd seen him somewhere.

Beside her, a hungry family filled five of the folding chairs. The three school-age boys needed haircuts but had clean hands, although the dirt under their fingernails betrayed the fact they'd washed in a hurry. Next to Burt's place sat a man who prided himself in his expansive knowledge of the school system. A principal? Superintendent? The woman beside him looked as if she'd rather be somewhere else and reminded Helen of her mother.

"Feels like a diner in New York," she joked with Burt.

"Except here—" He raised his voice to speak above the clatter and chatter. "Except here they're talking to each other." He reached for the salt and pepper.

Helen nodded at the slick-haired man across from her.

"You live here?" he asked her.

"I do!" The boy on her left in the faded t-shirt interrupted through a mouthful of potatoes.

Helen laughed and answered that she'd grown up in Rockwell but now worked in New York. From that point they easily traded information. The three men across from her were from the Chicago area and were on a business trip; the man on Burt's right actually was B. William Givens, head of the Rockwell school system; the boy next to her was Damien, who announced he was repeating third grade.

Although Burt shared only meager information about himself, he was wildly enthusiastic about the food and reached for his bowl of homemade apple cobbler before Helen finished her main course.

The Chicago men were cordial but seemed to be pumping Givens for the kind of news they couldn't get from a Chamber of Commerce brochure: "How do the people here feel about supporting the school corporation? . . . Do you have a drug problem in the schools? . . . Do your teachers stay or move on after a couple of years?"

Soaking up their conversation, Helen realized she was gleaning more information about her hometown than she'd picked up in the entire twelve weeks of her recovery period. Rockwell definitely was "on the ropes," Givens said, but observed that the folks in town had "terrific resiliency." He added that events like Comfort Food Day brought people together in a non-threatening setting and made the residents realize they were all working to maintain a quality community.

"We like the desserts here!" Damien scraped the bottom of his cobbler bowl. "Even better'n Mom's."

The three chuckled and reached for their wallets as Cherisse appeared with a basket brimming with money and jingling with change.

"Hey, Miss Helen, I heard you were here." Cherisse waited while the out-of-towners dug bills from their wallets. "Thanks. Thanks so much," she added when she saw the size of their contributions.

"Cherisse!" Helen felt as if she'd truly come home when her friend gave her a radiant smile. "I was going to call you tonight. Can you come over sometime so I can hear what you're up to?"

"Sure." Cherisse moved on down the line after she'd scrutinized Burt and signaled a quick thumbs-up to Helen.

"You sure you want to eat all that?" Burt surveyed the contents of her dessert bowl.

"You're out of luck. Best I ever had." She copied Damien's technique of circling the bowl with her spoon to get every trace of the cinnamon sauce.

"Well, look who's come all the way from New York." She felt a soft hand on her shoulder and was surprised to find Doris Lochschmidt behind her. When Helen and Burt struggled to stand in the cramped quarters to greet her, Doris motioned for them to stay seated.

"Hey there, Monty. Al. Good to see you again. Glad you finally found something else to eat in here besides French toast." They reached across the table to grasp her hand.

"This is my boss, Gordon Strunke. I think he's glad he made the trip with us today," the one named Monty replied.

"Always nice to meet another U of I grad." The man called Strunke gave Superintendent Givens an appreciative nod. "And all these other folks too, of course."

Helen could feel Doris squeezing her way between the

folding chairs behind her as she spoke.

"Kinda tight quarters, but I thought you'd like to see my son, Dougie. He says you and him were in the same class in school."

Helen knew a deep shade of magenta was washing over her face as she shook the hand of her high-school hero. All these years she'd wondered if he'd grown bald and flabby with a beer belly that reflected the numerous hours he'd spent in Rigoni's Uptown Tap. Instead, she found her hand encased in a rough but gentle grip that belonged to a dark blond hunk who looked as if he worked out daily.

"What's up?" When his blue eyes twinkled as they studied her appearance, she was at a loss for words.

"Uh . . ." was all she could manage.

"Her blood pressure, probably," Burt said to himself. "Hi. I'm Burt Meyer. I've heard a lot about you. And your mom." When he turned in his chair to shake Doris's hand, Helen could see that Burt was awed to be meeting Tommy Panczyk's sister.

Doug greeted them warmly and acknowledged the boys beside Helen. "Hey, dudes. I've got some work for you if you want to come over tomorrow morning."

"Epic!" Damien crowed. "Me'n my brothers live next to one of the houses Doug's workin' on. Sometimes he pays us for cleanin' up old shingles 'n crap," he explained to Helen.

"I've gotta keep moving," Doug said. "Or Mom'll get after me. This party of hers is a big deal." He stopped before he threaded his way through the chairs. "Hey, why don't the two of you join me'n my wife tomorrow night at Rigoni's? We can get caught up and talk about old times."

"Sounds great." As Helen felt her composure returning, she couldn't believe that she—well, she and Burt—had a date with Doug Lochschmidt.

"But I'll be over for a visit tomorrow afternoon, okay?" Doris grinned. "None of this Saturday-night nonsense at Rigoni's for me!"

Monty

The cobbler stuck in his throat. Damn! He should have been more proactive. Monty felt his skin tighten as he realized he should have arranged for Strunke to sit with members of the town council and chamber board. People who mattered—not folks like this rag-tag family with three starving unkempt boys and the couple from New York. None of them was a prominent citizen who could impress Strunke.

He began to relax a little when the school superintendent and his wife sat across from his boss; they might be able to contribute something positive. But dammit, Monty thought, he should have brought Strunke in for French toast on a quiet morning instead of gambling on a gathering crammed with a boisterous hodgepodge of residents.

He was glad to see Strunke bantering about the U of I with the superintendent, who'd introduced himself as Givens. But he wished his boss wouldn't waste so much time talking with that Damien kid. The boy was giving Strunke a pretty good earful of life in the third grade.

"You gonna eat that?" Damien asked, hopeful Strunke would give him his dessert.

"You bet." Strunke seemed to take it as a personal challenge and dug into his cobbler with zest.

God, Monty groaned to himself. This kid had the nerve to ask a stranger for the food off his plate! It's a wonder Strunke hadn't yelled at him. But sometimes his boss was hard to read.

Forcing down the rest of his dessert, he reflected on their afternoon together. Strunke had uttered one-word responses to the Chamber of Commerce rep who had walked them through the deserted cavernous Midwest facility. "Humph." That was it. Not a word about Rockwell's neighborhoods decked out in their fall colors or the fading business district that looked as if winter had already set in. Just "Humph."

Strunke had repeated it one more time when their tour was complete. Monty heartily thanked the rep and told him they'd be in touch. He knew their next communication would be through a polite rejection letter he'd have to draft. Al remained blessedly quiet for once.

After the three of them had piled back into the car, Strunke checked his cell then became more vocal. "I'm hungrier'n hell," he'd growled. "Let's go see what this food thing you've bragged up so much is all about."

Now Monty re-joined the table conversation as Strunke questioned the woman named Helen about growing up in Rockwell. He heaved a sigh of relief when she replied it was a good place to call home. The lawyer guy, who'd spent the evening neutralizing Al's trite line of patter, appeared even more enthusiastic.

"Great little town," the lawyer said. "Hey, I'd like to sit here and visit, but there are still people waiting for a seat.

Nice to have met you all."

Monty agreed and replied they needed to get moving too.

"God," Strunke sighed as they left the parking lot, "I haven't had a meal like that in years. Hey, Cooper, pull over here for a minute. I want to take one more look at this Midwest building."

Monty wished that Strunke had left well enough alone. In the eerie light of the rising harvest moon, the once-throbbing industrial heart of the town lay silent and ominous. He'd rather have his boss re-examine the building in broad daylight, not sit here in the dark like he was committing the size and shape of the building to memory.

"Okay." Strunke spoke with authority. "You can head for home now."

As Monty turned onto the highway, his boss confided, "You know, I grew up in a place like this. Bittersweet Heights, near Springfield. Had our own basketball team—I played point guard—and a lot of good folks. But something happened while I was at the U of I. The damn place just dried up and disappeared. Jobs were all in Springfield, the malls were in Springfield, and pretty soon all the young people moved to Springfield."

While Al snored softly in the back seat, Monty listened to a side of his boss he'd never known. Rambling in low tones, Strunke recalled his days in Bittersweet Heights:

"There was a time— I was about the age of that Damien kid—when I thought I'd never want to live anywhere else. Thought it was the perfect town . . . We watched out for each other. I couldn't get away with anything when I was growing up. Too many people eager to report back to my mom and dad . . . I didn't think there were still towns like mine around anymore. Hell, those were good folks in that restaurant tonight. Good food too . . . You say that old woman with the cane started the Comfort Food meals? Brilliant. Did you see how everyone got along? . . . And her brother was Tommy Panczyk? Unbelievable!"

Cruising up I-57 under the light of the orange moon, Monty absorbed Strunke's comments with non-committal answers. He'd planned to round off their day by giving his boss a strong sales pitch in favor of considering Rockwell as the location for their new plant. Instead, Strunke was doing all the talking—first a bit of monologue, then a few moments to weigh his own words, followed by more monologue and thoughtful silence.

When they pulled into the office parking lot, all three scrambled out of the car and stretched.

Strunke laughed, "Sure got a kick out of that boy. Damien. A dead ringer for me when I was that age. Dirty fingernails and all." His boss grew serious. "See me first thing tomorrow, both of you. And bring all your data. We need to put our heads together."

At 7:58 the following morning, the three met over cups of Lila's robust coffee in Strunke's office. Monty had never seen his boss so fired up.

"Gotta tell you. I liked what I saw last night. Spirit, that's what it was. Old-fashioned small-town spirit. The kind we had and should've kept in Bittersweet Heights."

Monty sipped his coffee so that Strunke couldn't see the smile that began to spread across his face.

"I'll tell you another thing I liked about Rockwell," Strunke continued. "Did you notice how all the signs around town were straight? Not a topsy-turvy one in the bunch. And the shrubs around the entrance off the highway and in the planters in the business district? Trimmed and well-kept."

Al started to speak, but Monty shook his head.

"A town can be on the ropes for awhile but still not lose its pride. That's what I saw—and that's what I felt at the dinner last night." Strunke nodded, satisfied he had summed up the situation.

"Mrs. Lochschmidt told me that Doug rehabs old houses and can't stand a crooked sign," Monty explained. "And her other son—Dirk, I think his name is—runs a nursery in Danville. He sees that the shrubs get trimmed when they need it."

"Whoever they are, they're doin' a helluva job." Strunke began to twist his ear. "Okay, boys. If we get moving, I think we can make this work. But both of you need to focus so we can get a scenario to corporate asap. If I'm behind it, I know they'll approve."

Monty felt his stomach churn with anticipation. He placed his mug on the conference table.

"You'll need about three months for the entire investigation process." Strunke twisted his lobe as he thought out loud. "We've got an empty building with more room than we'll need at first, right?"

Monty and Al nodded.

"And my first guess is we'll need to put about fifty

employees in there, including management, office, and production."

"If all goes well with the investigation," Monty figured, "then it shouldn't take more than a couple of weeks for the town board to give us incentive figures."

"After that, we'll need another couple of months to secure the building—either lease it or buy it." Al shifted from his early-morning coffee gear to practical business mode. "That'll take us up to—" he counted on his fingers— "to about March."

"Sounds right." Strunke swiveled in his chair. "What'll we need, Cooper—about three more months to equip?"

"If everything—everything goes according to plan." Monty felt as if he'd been spun around on the Tilt-a-Whirl at the fair back in Moline.

"Then we're looking at opening our new location in late June or early July." Strunke beamed. He raised his cup as if toasting. "Here's to Rockwell, boys. Better get moving."

Monty traded looks of disbelief with Al.

"Good thing I dated that girl in Bakers Corners," Al smirked, "or we'd never have stopped at The Boulder in the first place."

As Monty collected his papers and his now-bulging Rockwell folder, he heard Strunke congratulate himself with, "And I'm going to feel like I'm coming home every time I go there."

Helen

She felt so slammed after her first full day in Rockwell that she almost canceled out on their evening date with Doug and his wife. Before she even had a chance to reflect on the night before at The Boulder, she'd been trampled to a frazzle by the two hours she'd spent that morning with DeeDee Duley. Rockwell's leading real estate agent had insisted on exploring every crevice of the house.

When DeeDee leaned on the doorbell promptly at 9:30, Helen had been taken aback by the woman who stood before her, hand extended. The same height as Helen, she was about thirty pounds lighter with coal black shoulder-length hair that might have been attractive on someone twenty-five years younger. Her wide mouth and high cheekbones gave her a worn, haggard look, although she made a valiant attempt to compensate with her ankle-length Indian-print dress and noisy brass earrings that brushed her shoulders. Helen decided the woman must be going to a party later in the day and had dressed for it that morning.

Once DeeDee's boots crossed the front-door threshold, the woman became a non-stop adviser on décor:

"You need to purge, honey. You really need to purge . . . The place is big, but you've gotta rearrange some furniture so it doesn't seem so crowded. That stops a buyer quicker'n anything . . . And get rid of every family picture. Nobody wants to see someone else's relatives."

Helen informed her they'd already purged and taken down many family photos, but DeeDee shook her head so hard that her earrings clanged.

"Less is more, honey," she'd purred. "Less is more."

At last, when Helen was able to close the door behind the zealous agent, she looked at the gaudy business card in her hand and sighed.

"I dunno, Burt. I thought we made such progress." Glancing around the front hall she realized the enormity of the staging assignment DeeDee had given her. "Let's get out of here."

They opted for a sandwich and pie at The Boulder, where things had settled down to their usual soft drone. Back at the house, she considered indulging in a nap, but Doris popped in for "a minute" and stayed for two-and-a-half hours. Before she left, Doris peered out the kitchen window and suggested that her youngest son, Dirk, could spruce up the yard a bit.

"He's runnin' a big nursery in Danville now and knows how to fix things up without spendin' a bundle. Some of them bushes your folks planted years ago look a little out of control."

As Doris was leaving, Kristi phoned and said she and Pudge would like to bring supper to Helen's house the next evening. Helen was grateful they weren't coming today. One beer at Rigoni's was about all she was going to be able to handle. Burt, on the other hand, seemed energized by the people he'd met.

"And I thought Manhattan never slowed down." He grinned and grabbed their windbreakers to head for the pub. "This place is jumping. And without the traffic!"

"Welcome to Rockwell's real country club." Doug stood and waved them over to the square wooden table etched with names from the past. Grateful for Rigoni's smoke-free atmosphere, Helen still knew it would take her a few minutes to adjust to the stale odor of beer and the crush of noise. "My wife, Maria," he said with pride.

Helen was surprised by the warm, dimpled smile of the woman at his side. She'd been prepared for a Kardashian-type clone of Tonya from their high-school days, not this unaffected person whose blue eyes reflected her kind intelligence.

"Cherisse's 'matka.'" Helen could feel the exchange of mutual admiration as the two shook hands. "I've heard a lot about you."

"And I about you," Maria replied.

Helen hoped that Maria was not referring to tales of her dorky high-school days that Doug might have told her.

"All good," Maria hastened to add. "You have no idea how you've encouraged Cherisse."

From that moment, Helen felt herself relax. After a couple of beers, the four were laughing as Doug shared rarely repeated stories of his basketball cronies and Helen confessed she wished she had a group of high-school friends that she could gossip about now.

"I guess we'd need to call in my sister to tell us those." She hadn't meant to sound bitter but knew she'd tipped her hand on some of her true feelings.

"Nope." Doug drained his bottle. "I hate to be the one to tell you this, but Haley was old news by the time we started our senior year."

His statement stunned the group into silence. For a moment no one uttered a word.

When Doug blurted, "Sorry," Helen exploded with a laugh so liberating she could feel years of insecurity and resentment slide from her shoulders. Before they left at midnight, Maria insisted that Helen and Burt come to their house for supper on Wednesday night before their flight the next morning.

"Whad-ya know? I've got new friends. In Rockwell. Of all places!" Helen tried hard not to sound giddy as she and Burt made their way toward their car.

"Make that <u>old</u> new friends," she corrected herself with a slur and a giggle.

Burt rolled his eyes and opened her car door.

After they'd slept late the following morning, Helen told him, "I should feel like crap today, but I have more energy than usual. Let's have some coffee, and I'll take you on a tour before Cherisse comes over."

"Sounds good. Sure you're fit to drive? You put away the

beer faster than Doug and I did."

Finding no suitable retort, she picked up yesterday's newspaper and threw it at him. "I refuse to answer on the grounds . . . Yada yada yada."

Sometimes, she realized as she fired up the Altima, she missed the reassuring power of "Black Beauty." That old car had saved her life, and she'd always be grateful. Reflecting on that night in the blizzard, she felt as if it had happened several years ago. She'd been a different person then.

Guiding their rental through the streets of Rockwell, she was surprised by one observation: "This town's reversed itself," she told Burt. "A lot of rundown homes on the Sweet Briar side are in good shape, thanks to Doug Lochschmidt. But some of the beautiful mansions on the Longworth side are right out of a Charles Addams cartoon."

She looked both ways as she crossed the main highway, then turned down the one-lane slab of country pavement where her dad had taught her to drive. Haley had spent countless hours on these lonely roads with boyfriends who volunteered to show her how to shift gears and God-only-knew-what-else in their cars, but Helen always appreciated her dad's time and patience.

"Sorry we've missed the fields at their best," she apologized. "Everything's so brown and empty. Guess we'll have to come back next summer before the corn and beans are harvested."

"But your house will be—" Burt paused, cleared his throat, and switched to comments on the utter flatness of the terrain. When he speculated how far it might be to the water tower silhouetted against the deep blue sky in the distance, she chuckled.

"That's what's left of Bakers Corners. Six miles away."

"And we can see it without taking an elevator to the top of a skyscraper."

She knew he was talking to himself but appreciated his comparison. Viewing her home area through Burt's eyes gave her a new perspective.

"I'll take you there right now, then we'd better get back to the house. Cherisse'll be there before long."

She loved the response of the Altima as she floored the accelerator. "Black Beauty" may have been a classic but would never have had the zip to get them home as Cherisse was pedaling into the driveway.

"I could use a ten-speed like that in New York." Burt admired Cherisse's bike. "I'd probably get around a lot faster than I do in a cab."

"You might get run down too."

Helen laughed. Cherisse had never been short on realism. After Burt excused himself to watch pro football in the living room, Helen took her into the kitchen. There, over hot chocolate and coffee cake, they caught up on news.

Helen listened intently as she realized Cherisse had spread her wings in the last five months.

"I was at the Brickyard 400 when Ryan Newman won. Daddio and Matka let me take Ruby, and we really had fun . . . School isn't as bad as I thought it would be this year. We've got some new kids from Bakers Corners and Smithville. They're kinda shy, and me'n Ruby—I mean Ruby and I—have tried to make 'em feel at home . . . My English teacher's new. At first she wondered why I wrote about NASCAR, and I told her that's what I liked. She gave

me a funny look, then she smiled and said that was okay . . .
Me 'n Ruby—Ruby and I—got picked to go to the U of I for
a workshop next month . . . I've been helping Grando a lot at
the Comfort Food Days. She won't tell nobody—anybody—
but those dinners really wear her out. Ruby comes with me
sometimes, but you know how Grando is. She thinks nobody
can do things the way she can—not even Darcy and Tiffany.
She's sure stubborn. And she says I'm just like her."

When Cherisse pulled on her hoodie and prepared to
leave, Helen reminded her that she and Burt were looking
forward to supper at her house on Wednesday night.

"That's what I heard." Cherisse's face clouded. "I'm so
mad that I can't be there, but Ruby's folks asked me to go to
a concert in Champaign with them that night." She paused,
giving Helen a straight look. "Promise me you won't talk
about me with my parents, okay? It's—well, it's—" she
glanced away. "Sometimes I tell you stuff I don't tell anybody else."

"Got it." Helen hugged her once, then again. "You're my
special friend, Cherisse. You know stuff about me too that
I've never told anyone else, so we've got a deal."

A sobering thought struck Helen as she watched Cherisse
hop on her bike and pedal to the street: How would she
get along without these chats every few months? After all,
Cherisse was the only one she'd ever told about how miserable she'd been as the "Other Twin" when she and Haley
were growing up. Cherisse, at her tender age, had understood.
Helen doubted that anyone—not even Burt—would get it.

"What time are Pudge and Kristi coming over?" Burt's
call from the living room interrupted her thoughts.

"About 6."

"Late. By Midwest standards—" The rest was blanketed by the blaring of NFL halftime scores and endless analysis.

Two hours later Burt was intrigued as Kristi lifted the foil from a taco casserole she had brought and set out a large tossed salad and rolls.

"We'll eat at the kitchen table," Helen told them.

"Is there any other place?" Pudge's grin bunched his freckles together and lit up his face. Helen was glad to have this opportunity to share another meal with the couple who'd been her mainstays while she recuperated, the two who saw her at her worst, and still wanted to bring her a meal.

When evening shadows fell across the table as Pudge dished out full plates, Helen switched on the lights.

"Days is gettin' shorter," Pudge observed. "In two weeks we have to turn back our clocks, then it'll really get dark early."

"I hate to see winter come," Kristi said sadly.

As they exchanged small talk, Helen realized they sounded like people who'd known each other for years. Pudge and Kristi spoke of their son's surprise marriage and how thrilled Mason and his bride were to be fixing up Pudge's mom's house. Pudge grumbled about Jenna's decision to break up with Noah and figured she robbed him of a dependable son-in-law. Both were grateful for the amount of rehab work that Doug had thrown Pudge's way.

"It's still tough without a steady job. I keep lookin' and hopin', but so far nothing's turned up." He transferred a hefty helping of salad onto his plate.

Helen exchanged quick looks with Burt, each knowing

they could never quite empathize with Pudge's state of uncertainty.

"You two never have to worry about that, do you?" Pudge focused on his casserole.

"Not much, but we do get stressed out." Burt stopped eating. "Helen's got writers and editors breathing down her neck, and I've got—well, I've got a couple of clients you wouldn't believe."

"I know you're going through a hard time, Pudge, but I want you to know how much I appreciate all you did to clean out the house and get it shaped up," Helen reassured him.

Suddenly self-conscious as the others trained their attention on him, Pudge took an extended drink from the soda bottle Helen had remembered to put at his place.

"Well, both of you," Helen quickly added. "You had so many good ideas—and I loved your suggestions."

That was all Kristi needed to plunge into her plan for "what I would do if this was my house." She spoke of painting the kitchen cupboards and told them about fabrics she had seen that would be perfect for covering the living room furniture. "And I'd get rid of that lavender carpet. That's the first thing I'd do."

Helen stifled a giggle. "Me too," she agreed. "I've felt that way for a long time." She studied Kristi with a fresh perspective. "So, tell me. What would you do upstairs? Let's go take a look."

They toured the four bedrooms, and Kristi laid out her plans for each, stating more than once that she wanted the place "to feel homey."

Later, over brownies and ice cream, Helen told her

fondly, "You've spent a lot of time here. I could tell—even last winter when I was such a grouch—that you love this house."

Kristi blushed and dug her fork into her brownie. "I used to make fun of Pudge's mom 'cause she thought it was such a beautiful place. Then, after I knew it from the inside out, I kinda started to feel the same way."

"I'll talk this over with Burt and see how much he thinks I can afford to have done before I put it on the market." Helen sighed. "And I'll see what kind of price DeeDee Duley wants me to ask for it."

As they discussed other topics, Helen was grateful that her sister was more than a thousand miles away. Haley would be content to get by with few if any improvements and would pump up the price as high as possible. The thought of her twin made Helen tremble.

"You cold?" Pudge wondered.

"Just a shiver. Must have been the idea of winter coming." Helen glanced away. "Or the ice cream."

Helen had always felt frenzied and unsettled in New York when she faced approaching deadlines and increasing demands. But she was startled when she wakened on Monday morning—in her own bed, in her own room, in her home town—to find herself smothered by that same suffocating feeling. Too many people to see! Too many decisions to make! Too little time and not a moment for herself! Quietly, she crept out of bed.

"You tossed all night long." Burt pulled up the covers and moved to the center of the bed.

In the kitchen, she punched the button on the coffee pot and debated about turning on the heat. The chill from the frost during the night had seeped into the house. Lord, she thought, if the furnace doesn't come on, I'll need to call someone right away. Her anxiety peaked again but subsided when the familiar roar erupted from the basement, signaling warmth was on the way—at least for the day. She tugged her robe around her, filled her mug with black coffee, and began to scribble out a list. If she saw her tasks on paper, she could organize her chores and scare away the pressure monster inside her.

She had three days before she and Burt left. Today, she'd visit her dad and check with DeeDee to see if she had an asking price in mind for the house. Helen had told Kristi to have Jenna stop in after lunch before she went to work, and Cherisse had asked if she could bring Ruby over to look at all the changes in the house. That would take care of today. Tomorrow would fill itself up.

When Burt came downstairs and suggested he make pasta and homemade sauce for supper, the anxiety monster inside her vanished. Burt always seemed to sense when she needed him most. Once again, she took a deep breath and began her day.

She was pleased to find her dad had been shaved and seemed a little more alert than usual. Later, DeeDee gave her an asking figure higher than she'd expected and would allow her some wiggle room on the price of the house. Helen approved when she saw Jenna had restored her hair to its natural auburn and was spilling over with excitement about the nursing scholarship she received.

"Dad doesn't seem to realize that Noah and I were so over each other a long time ago," she'd told Helen. "When Noah said it was stupid to go to Chicago for the same training I could get in Danville, I knew for sure I couldn't spend my life with him."

Feeling her energy ebbing when Cherisse and Ruby burst in after school, Helen asked Cherisse to give Ruby a tour of the house. Over cups of hot chocolate, she wished she could tap into some of their zeal as they discussed their school projects and the homecoming float they would help with the following weekend.

"Lord, I'm bushed," she confessed to Burt after the girls left. "I owe you big time for making the homemade meal."

"Cooking's my therapy . . . allows me time to think." He twirled strands of spaghetti around his fork. "I've been wondering. Where are you going to stay when you come back to see your dad? You'll still want to do that a couple of times a year. At least."

"I don't know. There's the Moonlight Motel on the edge of town. It's been there as long as I can remember."

She didn't want to talk about it. Savoring Burt's special sauce and having a quiet evening at home were enough. She took a bite of garlic bread and changed the subject.

"Lord, I wish Pudge could find a steady job! When I see Kristi and him here, I feel as if they're the ones who grew up in the house. Not me." She speared a piece of lettuce, appreciating the fact that Burt had made a salad too. "Really good," she told him.

Amazed that he seemed so at ease in her house as he refilled their wine glasses, she wished that Burt had come to Rockwell long ago. Finally, he pushed his empty plate aside and rubbed his chin. She'd seen him do that often over the years before he had something important to say.

"I have an idea. It's complicated, I know, so bear with me." His brown eyes locked on hers. "Haley wants her money out of the house. Like yesterday, right?"

She nodded.

"You've made good investments over the years. Why don't you use some of your money and buy her out?" He put his fingers to his lips to let Helen know he didn't want her to interrupt. "That way, you can get her off your case and do whatever you damn well please with the place."

"I never gave it a thought . . ." Her voice trailed off as she considered the scenario. Eventually, she'd get her money back when she sold the house. Things would feel a lot simpler without pesky calls from Haley.

When he assured her they could take DeeDee's appraisal, cut it in half, and make the offer to Haley, she saw the possibilities. She knew if she told Haley it was a good opportunity to get her portion of the house money without having to wait any longer, her sister would jump at the chance. All good! Yet, she, Helen, would be the sole owner. It would be her own hard-earned savings that would be poured into it, and she'd be the one left holding the bag if the house didn't sell.

"I—I don't know—" She began to waver. "We're not certain we can find a buyer—"

"Hear me out." Burt leaned on his forearms and began to outline his plan. "You love this place more than you want to admit. Right?"

"Well—"

"And I fell for it the first afternoon I stepped into the front hall. The way the light hit that beautiful woodwork." He paused as he remembered. "I think there are a couple of other people who love this house as much as we do. And they're right under our nose."

At first she didn't comprehend. Where was Burt going with this? Then she sat bolt upright.

"Pudge and Kristi?" He couldn't be serious.

"Pudge and Kristi." He nodded and smiled.

"But they—" Doubts swirled through her head. "They don't have any money. And they—" Breathlessly she spilled out her concerns that the house was too big and their bank account too small.

"I'm not saying it'll work." She could see Burt begin to backpedal. "But if I were you, I'd want to talk with them before I listed it."

"I—I—" Not often had she been speechless with Burt. "I'm not sure where to begin."

He raised his glass. "First things first. Give Haley a call tomorrow and see if she'd like her money. That'd be a good place to start."

Although outlandish dreams involving the house haunted her all night, Helen felt rejuvenated the next morning when she came downstairs to breakfast. She and Burt skirted the subject as they ate bacon and eggs and savored the rich, dark coffee. Finally, she rinsed their plates and announced, "I'm calling Haley."

When Burt reminded her that Haley was in a different time zone and might just be getting out of bed, Helen shot back, "Good time to catch her."

She grabbed a piece of paper and listed all the benefits in her sister's favor, in case Haley pelted her with negative responses. Geared for battle, she punched in her sister's cell.

When Haley answered, she was downright cheery because she had a red-hot prospect lined up for a condo showing that morning. Launching into her prepared spiel, Helen was stunned when Haley cut her off.

"Am I hearing you right? You're saying you wanta buy me out?"

"Looks like the simplest way." Helen tried to keep her voice steady. "You'll have your money and—"

"Whatever. Sounds good to me. What's the appraisal price?"

When Helen repeated it, Haley questioned, "And I get half? In a few days?"

"As soon as possible." Helen resisted the urge to remind her sister that, after all, Haley was the realtor and knew more about this than Helen did.

Haley gave her a fax number to speed up the paperwork process.

"Sounds good. I can use the do-re-mi. See ya."

When Helen heard the click, she realized her twin had not said thanks or asked about their dad.

"Done!" she exclaimed and threw her arms around Burt. "Lord, I feel shaky. But do I feel good."

Burt seemed preoccupied as he hugged her. "Then it's time to think about the next step." He filled her coffee cup. "What—what's that?" She eased into her chair. "I need to see my lawyer so we can get that paperwork faxed to Haley."

Slowly, he began to build his case for talking frankly with Pudge and Kristi to see if they had any interest in the house. "Soon—but with no pressure, if you know what I mean."

"Like this afternoon?"

"Today's Tuesday already, and we're leaving Thursday. If they're out of the picture, that'll give you tomorrow to line up a listing with DeeDee."

"Maybe they can come over after Kristi gets off work at the school. I'd still love for us to go to Danville to Steak 'n Shake tonight. But only if we have time."

"Then get a move on, woman," Burt flashed a mischievous smile.

She barely had time to grab a protein bar as she churned through the rest of the day. Her lawyer said he'd have the papers ready to fax to Haley the next morning and reminded Helen to transfer the necessary amount from her investment fund into her New York checking account. Both Pudge and Kristi sounded curious when they agreed to stop by the house around three. Helen squeezed in a few minutes with her dad and told him she'd see him the next morning, although she knew he wouldn't remember. Then she dashed to the grocery to pick up chocolate chip cookies and cream soda. Throughout the day the appraisal and asking price weighed heavily on her mind.

"I can't ask Pudge and Kristi to pay so much for a house

that still needs a lot of work," she lamented to Burt when she arrived home. "But I think if I cut it back thirty thousand, they might be able to do it."

"Good God, Helen! You'd be losing money on the deal." He threw down his magazine and roared up from her dad's La-Z-Boy. "You can't afford to do that."

"Maybe I can't afford *not* to." She felt calm, almost serene when she explained that the house had been in her family for almost sixty years and needed the perfect people to move into it. "I'd at least like to try to make that happen."

She had Kristi's tea water boiling when the doorbell rang.

"Just us," Pudge announced as he opened the door.

"Come on in." Her heart raced as she led them into the kitchen. "I have a lot to talk with you about."

"I know, I know." Ignoring his cream soda, Pudge seemed jittery. Kristi poured water over a tea bag but hadn't said a word. "There's still all that work upstairs you need to show me before you leave." He drew a deep breath. "But first, Kristi and me—we want to tell you something."

Helen's mind jumped ahead. Were they in deeper financial trouble than she'd realized? Was Jenna having second thoughts about going to Chicago for her nurses' training? Or Mason—was something going on with him?

"Sure." She tried to sound composed. "Shoot."

Pudge looked at Kristi. "Me 'n her—well, her 'n me— we'd like to buy the house," he blurted. "But first we need to know what you're asking."

Dumbstruck, Helen put down her coffee before she dropped it. "The house," she echoed. "<u>This</u> house?"

Pudge rushed ahead. "Yep. And we think we've got it all

figured out. If we can get a loan from my brother Red in Key
West for a down payment, we could prob'ly swing it."

"Uh . . ." she replied. She glanced at Burt as figures raced
through her head. Appraisal price? A special discount? Burt
fidgeted.

"We know real estate isn't movin' too fast here in town
right now but still—"

"What Pudge is going to say is that it'd be a dream come
true for us." Kristi's soft words were barely audible. "We've
grown to love the place."

"But—" Helen sputtered.

"We know all the reasons we shouldn't move here. It's
too big for us, too much money for us. Doesn't make good
business sense at all," Kristi continued.

"We'll need time," Helen began, "to talk about price.
And dates. I'm asking—" Again she looked at Burt. "I'm
asking one-hundred-forty thousand." She saw Burt relax.
"And no rush."

"Just please don't say no right off the bat." Kristi's
request was earnest.

"We'll work it out. One way or another." Helen wished
she felt more in control, but their desire for the house had
thrown her for a loop.

"Hey," Pudge lifted his soda bottle and said, "You mentioned you needed to talk to us about something."

"I—" Helen felt tears welling up inside. "I—"

"She was going to ask you two if you might be interested
in buying the house," Burt finished for her. "How's that for
timing?"

"I'll be right back." Helen excused herself and headed

for the bathroom. There, she dissolved in grateful tears as the burden of selling the house began to slide from her shoulders. Somehow, the four of them would make this work. She flushed the toilet so that no one would guess she'd fallen apart, then peered in the mirror, wiped her blotchy face, and returned to the kitchen.

Over cookies and endless cups of coffee, tea, and soda, they discussed the price. Helen advised them that the house had been appraised at one-hundred-fifty thousand dollars, but repeated that she would take one-hundred-forty, an offer available only to the two of them.

Burt casually introduced the option of a land contract that would make it easier for them to buy the house without getting an additional loan from Red or anyone. The down side for the two of them would be that if they couldn't make payments, the house would revert to Helen. Pudge chewed his lip and said he understood how it worked.

Before they left, they agreed to return the next afternoon at three to discuss financial particulars. They also promised not to share the news of the impending sale or any of its details with others.

"And I'll fix that faucet on the kitchen sink so it won't drip," Pudge added.

After she closed the door behind them, Helen felt her joy erupt.

"Can you believe it?" She couldn't resist twirling in a circle. "Can you absolutely believe it?"

"Don't celebrate till you've received the first payment," Burt cautioned.

"I know, I know." She giggled. "But we can still head to

Danville for chili mac at Steak 'n Shake. I haven't had that since I was in high school."

"You treating?" he asked with a wry grin.

"You bet." She beamed. "But you'd better drive. I'm feeling a little shaky."

The next day the sun dazzled the orange maple trees that lined the streets of Rockwell as Helen completed her list of errands. Looking forward to supper with Doug and Maria, she enjoyed a mid-morning visit with her dad, stopped at The Boulder to pick up a carry-out order of potato soup for lunch, and listened with gratitude as Burt ran through the financial figures that Pudge and Kristi would need to approve if they decided to proceed with a land contract.

"That chili mac sure gave me heartburn all night long." Burt rubbed his stomach. "I think I'm ready to get back to the Thai food in Manhattan."

"Oh, that's even worse," she protested. "The chili mac was every bit as good as I remembered."

She was pleased to see that Pudge and Kristi seemed eager and animated when they arrived. The four reviewed Burt's projections, then Pudge insisted on fixing the kitchen faucet. When they prepared to leave, his face grew serious.

"I hope you understand we can't sign anything today. We don't do this kind of thing every day, and I want someone at the bank to look it over real good and tell us it's okay. I mean, with my situation and all—"

"How about two weeks?" Helen suggested. "And if you

need more time, let me know." She noticed how longingly Kristi glanced around the room. "We all want to make this work."

That evening, Helen's thoughts strayed to the sale of the house as they entered the two-story home that Doug and Maria had remodeled at the edge of town. Helen remembered coming here when she was in fifth grade. She and her mom had brought some clothes to be altered. Back then a heavy coal oil odor from the stove in the living room permeated the home, and the linoleum that ran through the house was thin and showed patches of floorboards in a few bare spots. She'd been fascinated that the sewing lady who lived here stuffed her mouth full of pins and never seemed to swallow any.

But now, all that had changed. Her stomach growled when she inhaled the fragrance of a home-cooked meal—she couldn't identify it—when she and Burt stepped into the kitchen.

"Umm—smells delicious." She handed her jacket to Maria.

"Polish dinner," Maria replied. "We thought you could use a solid meal before you put yourselves into the hands of the airlines tomorrow."

"Great house," Burt marveled. "You've obviously done some work on it."

"Got that right." Doug's dimples deepened as he smiled and shrugged. "It's what I do. Come on. We'll show you around."

Helen was awed to think this had been the sewing lady's eerie house. Warmth and cheery colors brightened the home, but even more so, the feeling that people who loved each other lived here exuded from every corner.

"We're sorry Cherisse can't be here tonight," Helen commented after they'd made a loop through the upstairs bedrooms. They'd paused to study the photos of NASCAR heroes and Taylor Swift taped on Cherisse's walls.

"She was bummed about that too." Doug stopped to straighten a picture of Kevin Harvick. "But Ruby's folks bought those tickets two months ago and paid a fortune for them."

At the table, conversation flowed easily as they scooped sausage, potatoes, and cabbage onto their plates. Maria seemed intrigued with the lives Helen and Burt led in Manhattan—how they commuted to work and what they did for fun on weekends. She asked detailed questions about the theater scene and current off-Broadway shows.

"I lived there for a short time myself." Her voice took on a wistful tone, and Helen saw Doug watching her with concern. When Helen pressed her for more details, Maria jumped up and announced it was time for dessert.

"Have to admit I cheated on this." Her voice seemed too bright. "I asked Doris to make one of her lemon meringue pies."

"Oh, Lord! I'm going to gain so much weight that the airline may charge me double tomorrow," Helen complained happily. "You really shouldn't have."

"But we're really glad you did." Burt trained his attention on the pie as Maria's knife sliced through the flaky

213

crust that held the tart filling and airy meringue. "Doug, I've learned in one week that your mom's cooking puts our New York chefs to shame."

"There's none better, that's for sure," Doug agreed. "And I was lucky enough to grow up on it. Back in those days though, we ate a lot of casseroles and home-canned veggies. Mom had to pinch her pennies when all of us were home."

"Your mom is quite a lady." Helen looked into the face of her former heart throb and realized she could now talk to him without stammering. "She's the one who coached me through the recovery from my accident. The rehab team kept forcing me on, and Pudge was always there to encourage me, but it was Doris who told me again and again, 'If I could do it, so can you.'"

She stopped and swallowed hard. "Quite a lady," she repeated.

"We almost lost her, you know. Came so damn close." Doug put down his fork. "And all my fault. All my fault."

"Doug, don't!" Maria chided, then went on to tell how Doug's boat, the pride of his life, hit a steel pier one night and his mom and other family members had been thrown into Lake Michigan. It was a miracle that a boater spotted them and was able to rescue them. But it was his oldest brother Denny who had saved their mom. Surgeries and months of rehab restored her quality of life, Maria said.

"Damn Denny," Doug muttered. "Always a shithead, but he came through when she needed him." He sighed. "Thank God."

"Language, Kochany. Language," Maria reminded him.

Helen saw by the loving glance the two exchanged that

Doug, legendary wild rascal of her high-school days, had been tamed at last. And he didn't mind at all.

"You probably don't know the word, 'Kochany.' It's a Polish term of endearment," Maria explained.

"Next time we're here, the meal's on us," Burt promised as he and Helen said their goodbyes. They drove in contented silence back to her house. Before getting out of the car to go inside, Burt said softly, "I wonder what Maria's New York story is. Something she obviously doesn't want to talk about."

"Maybe someday she'll tell us." Helen wondered too. "When the time is right."

Monty

During the few weeks that followed their visit to Comfort Food Day, Monty felt as if he'd been split into three different people. There was Monty-on-a-Mission, who was dedicated to quickly amassing the necessary information for the new GRN plant in Rockwell. There was New Nonchalant Monty, who suddenly had scrapped his revered daily schedule. Finally, there was Bewildered Monty, who constantly struggled to cope with Theo's crisis and his rejection of all the goals Monty had set for him.

He embraced the challenge that Gordon Strunke had handed him and executed the steps of the Rockwell investigation process with crisp efficiency. He learned to shrug when leaders of his local civic groups questioned his lack of enthusiasm, especially when he declined the nomination for the presidency of his Rotary Club. But the constant burden of trying to deal with Theo's newly claimed identity gnawed on him until he felt like a feather tossed in the wind. He'd never realized how much he'd pinned his own self-worth on his son's athletic success.

It was Claire who pointed that out to him as they finished

their dinner on the patio picnic table. Although he was grateful for the balmy Indian summer evening, he felt a wave of melancholy wash over him as he recalled the bonfires he'd shared as a preteen with his neighborhood buddies who'd spilled out of their nearby homes to toast marshmallows. God, how he missed the aroma of burning leaves on a night like this!

"You're quiet," she observed as she slipped her hand over his.

He sighed and said nothing, wishing he could remind her that if she hadn't kept those damn pills, Theo wouldn't have taken them and if he hadn't taken them, they wouldn't have suffered such a shattering change in their lives. And if . . . and if . . . and if . . . But he knew he could never play that card. Claire herself was seeing their counselor for individual sessions to help her deal with that guilt.

"I know you've got a lot on your plate at work right now," she continued sympathetically, "but I also know that the basketball thing with Theo is still eating away at you." She shook away a lock of blond hair from her face. "It was kind of like Theo's success on the court would validate your own career at Northwestern." She glanced away. "I don't know. I just don't know anymore."

Monty was stung by her comments. "That sounds like something Len Vogel might've told you." God, sometimes he hated their counselor. It was as if he pried some of their darkest thoughts loose and brought them out into the sun for everyone to examine.

"Maybe," she agreed.

He considered her words and wondered if they might

contain a tiny speck of truth. Sure, he loved reliving his own triumphs on the court through Theo's efforts, but he really didn't need to have his son succeed in order to feel successful himself. Or did he?

He tried switching the subject to his work on the Rockwell project.

"I realize I'm preoccupied. Lots of paperwork. Extra trips to Rockwell. And I'm sorry about that. I truly am." He noticed her eyes were moist. "I want to get it right, Claire. I just want to get it right."

"And *we* need to get it right, Monty. You and I." She brushed away a tear. "We had such different dreams for Theo. We've talked about that with Len. But he told us something that's really stuck with me—that it's okay for us to mourn that person we lost."

Her words brought Monty to life as abruptly as if she'd poured a bucket of cold water on him.

"Thank God we didn't <u>really</u> lose him!" He stood and walked around the picnic table. "Thank God for that," he whispered.

"True. But we did lose that person we'd created the moment he was born. Remember? He was going to be our perfect son—good student, which he is; outstanding Boy Scout, which didn't work out too well; and basketball player for Northwestern. We had it all planned, Monty."

"We sure did." He crunched through the carpet of orange and yellow maple leaves that surrounded their table. "And I learned the hardest lesson of my life," he continued bitterly. "You can make all the plans you want, but things change. People change. Even our kids—and we—change!"

"I always hoped Cass would become a ballet dancer." Claire bit her lip to keep it from trembling. "And now look what's happened. <u>She's</u> the one on the volleyball and basketball courts."

"And Theo—oh God, Claire—" He felt tears streaming down his cheeks. "I am so mixed up. I'm—I'm grateful we still have him. I can't say that enough. But I'm not sure I'll ever get used to the fact that our son wants to dance. And that he likes—likes boys."

She stood and enfolded him in her arms while he cried out his grief.

"We had an awful wake-up call, Monty. Both of us were immersed in our own worlds. Especially me, I think."

He sniffed and recalled the tight schedule he had designed as his path to success—forcing himself through rigorous physical workouts, grabbing every opportunity to take on more civic leadership responsibilities, shoving everything <u>he</u> wanted for his son down Theo's throat. He tried to talk but could find no words.

"We've been spared the grief of true loss, Monty." Claire spoke for him.

"And now we have a boy we don't even know." He pictured his blond son, soaring on stage to Tchaikovsky. Searching Claire's eyes for an answer, he added. "But we will. I promise."

"And we'll be gentle as we begin to find out who he is." She snuggled comfortably into his arms.

"That also sounds like something else Len Vogel might have preached," he kidded tenderly.

She broke away and gave him one of her brilliant smiles

that reminded him of the days when they first started dating.

"Don't you forget it. You and I've got a lot of learning ahead of us, Monty. Let's do it together and see where it takes us."

PART III

2014

Pudge

Late January

He nibbled on a ham salad sandwich, then dropped it back on his plate. The cream soda seemed extra strong today, so he left it on the counter. He'd come in early to avoid the lunch crowd and promised Doug he'd be back to do some painting by 12:30.

Shoot, he thought; he hadn't felt this dumpy since the day of his mom's funeral. His phone conversation with Helen the night before had tied his gut into a bunch of knots that tightened every time he thought of it.

Helen had been so good to him, almost always kind and chatty even when she was recovering from her accident last winter. But when he blurted that he and Kristi had decided against buying her house on a land contract, he hit a wall of silence.

"You what?" she'd finally asked in disbelief.

"I—um—I said Kristi and me think we better not take you up on your offer." When no reply came, he added, "You know—to buy the house. I'm—I'm just so sorry."

He scrambled for words. "Kristi's been up cryin' for nights now—can't sleep for fear we're biting off more'n we can chew. Financially, that is."

"But I thought we had it all planned," Helen protested.

"Me too. So did Kristi." He took a deep breath. "Then she started thinkin'. All of a sudden everything seemed too big to her—the size of the house, the amount of money we could lose if we can't make all the payments . . . I'm sorry."

"But I thought she loved the house—"

"Oh, she did. She does. That's what makes this so hard." He'd run out of words.

The awkward silence that followed made him squirm. Jiminy, he wished she'd yell at him. Say something. Anything. After a few moments he thought he could hear Helen wilting on the other end of the line.

"Oh, Pudge."

"It's not what we want. It's—it's just the way things are." The phone was damp from his clammy hand when he'd set it back on its charger.

Now, as he reviewed every word of his conversation with Helen, he felt worse by the minute. He took a bite of a potato chip and tried the cream soda again. They must've put an extra dose of fizz in this batch at the bottling company. He sighed. He sure missed his mom. She would've had some wise words to make him feel better.

"Looking for company?"

At first Pudge didn't respond to the request and continued moving his soda bottle around in circles on the counter.

"Okay if I sit here?" the voice asked.

Pudge looked up and saw that fellow Monty taking the

stool next to him. All dressed up in a sport coat and looking confident. The last person Pudge wanted for trading small talk.

"Sure," he lied.

"Monty Cooper." The guy stuck out his hand. "We've met before."

"Yep," was all Pudge could manage.

"Saw you a couple of months ago at Comfort Food Day," Cooper reminded him. He ordered a meat loaf special and then turned his full attention on Pudge.

"You okay today? It is Pudge, isn't it?"

He nodded. "Yeah. Got some—whad'ya call 'em— issues. Yeah, issues. They're bugging me. Didn't realize it showed." He wished this guy would find another place to sit.

"Oh, God, I know all about issues." Cooper drained the glass of water Tiffany placed in front of him. "You name one, I've had it."

They sat quietly for a few minutes before Cooper shot another question in Pudge's direction. "You used to work at Midwest, right?"

"Right." Pudge felt his shoulders droop even more. Another reminder of things not going his way.

"Then I'm going to share something with you," Cooper confided. "The reason I'm in Rockwell today."

"On your way to Danville again, I s'pose." Pudge could hear the flatness in his own voice.

"Not a chance. I have a meeting this afternoon with <u>your</u> town board. My company's been looking all over several states for a new site. We're ready to check out the incentives your board's willing to offer us." Cooper pushed a forkful of meat loaf into his mouth. "Umm."

"You're shittin'—I mean kidding—me?" Pudge sat, frozen to his stool, afraid to believe the words he had heard.

Cooper grinned and assured him, "I'd never do that."

Pudge felt his shoulders lift. "I'll keep your news to myself."

He checked his watch, startled to see that it was 12:20. "I've gotta go," he said. "Promised Doug I'd be back at the house at 12:30." He zipped his plaid wool jacket and offered his hand to Cooper. "That was a heckava lunch. Glad we could sit together."

"Me too. Wish me luck."

Trying to appear nonchalant, Pudge gave Cooper a thumbs-up and braced himself for the arctic air that would greet him when he opened the door. But as he started his truck and waited for it to warm up, he pounded his steering wheel and shouted in the privacy of his cab, "Jobs! Goll-dern!"

Monty

He'd never seen anyone so ecstatic over the possibility of a new plant. Pondering that thought as he cleaned the last of the meat loaf and mashed potatoes from his plate, he heard a familiar sound behind him and knew Doris Lochschmidt was approaching.

"Hi, there." She greeted him like an old friend. "Got time for a piece of pie? It's on me." She cocked her head and waited for his reply.

"Sure—if it really is on you." He was glad he knew her well enough to make a joke. "Pull up a stool." He patted the seat next to him.

"Naw. Let's go back to my booth. More comfortable there." She turned before he could answer and was on her way, taking longer strides than usual. Monty sensed she was on a mission.

As they slid across the blue seats, Monty peeked at his watch.

"You got time before your meeting at 2." When Tiffany approached, Doris called, "Coffee and those two pieces of lemon meringue that I saved."

"How did you know I have a meeting?" God, he thought, this woman is a walking sponge.

"I got my ways." Grinning impishly, she added. "I don't come to The Boulder just to bake a pie now and then, you know." She nodded, thanked Tiffany, then grew serious. "I've been thinkin' about somethin' that I need to talk with you about."

His mind leapfrogged ahead as he tried to imagine her concern. Certainly he couldn't share any confidential information about the GRN deal.

"Sure." He tried not to let his hesitation show.

"I like your son. Theo, isn't it?" Her eyes bore into him.

"Right." God, he wondered, what does Theo have to do with Doris Lochschmidt?

"He sure makes me think of my brother, Tommy. When you brought Theo in here last summer, I wanted to stare at him. Same sweet smile. Same manner. Made me wonder if he plays the piano."

"Nope." As Monty cut through the layers of meringue, lemon filling, and light-as-a-cloud crust, he couldn't believe he was lucky enough to be eating this piece of pie with the lady who'd baked it. "He's decided to dance." He took a deep breath. "Rather than play basketball."

"Broke your heart too, didn't it?"

"Well—" He hated to open his bag of pain to someone he barely knew.

"That's what happened to us, to my family." She put down her fork and stared into space as she recalled her younger brother. She told Monty about the time her sister, Violet, splurged the money she'd earned cleaning houses to buy a used piano from Dr. Dawes. "Then my friend Kate—well, her dad paid for lessons so Tommy could learn from a real good teacher in Danville." Her pie sat neglected as she remembered how most folks in town expected Tommy to be a basketball player "like Vic and Charley."

"But he'd have nothin' to do with it. I had a shit-for-brains brother-in-law who lived with us who said Tommy'd be a queer if we didn't start makin' him play basketball."

Monty winced at the word but kept listening, fascinated by the tale of Tommy Panczyk's life. Doris told him Tommy didn't care, that he took all the verbal abuse and went to New York after graduation.

"My mom knew in her heart he was gay, but when he told her one Christmas, it about did her in. We all hung our heads—like he was a criminal or somethin'—then Mom lit into us. She wrote letters to Vic and Lorene, who lived too far away to come home, and talked to me'n Violet and Charley like we were first-graders. Asked us if he was the same brother we'd always loved, and we said yes. Asked us if we were proud of him gettin' a few jobs here and there as a piano player in New York, and we said yes again."

She stopped to reflect on her past.

"I'll never forget that talk she gave us at her kitchen table. I was tryin' to keep my three oldest kids out of her cupboards while I nursed Dougie. And I was pregnant again. Can you believe it?" She smiled and shook her head.

"My mom explained that Tommy had never changed. It was us who'd changed 'cuz we'd found out somethin' about him we hadn't known for sure. Tommy didn't need to do anything different. We all needed to shape up. She didn't mince words neither!"

Monty washed down his last bite with black coffee and squeezed his eyes so the tears wouldn't trickle down his cheeks. Finally, as Doris finished her own pie, he admitted, "It sure isn't easy."

"Never easy when you're different. Me? I was poor growin' up. Tommy was gay. You probably weren't poor growin' up, but there had to be times when you felt different from other kids. And now you've got a boy—a sweet, wonderful, talented boy—who's gay. And you're still hurtin' 'cause you wanted him to play basketball."

"I—I'm not sure what to do," Monty admitted.

"First of all, stop bein' selfish and feelin' sorry for yourself. Theo's got a dream. He's gonna have a different life than you and your wife had planned. But—" she held her cup for Tiffany to refill, "you gotta get on board."

"Thank you."

"You're gonna have some real happy moments with that kid," she promised. "And there'll be times when he's performing he'll knock you and your wife right out of your seats."

"You think so?"

"I know so. Now go kick ass at that town board meeting!"

Helen

Early February

She'd let her frustration fly the week before when she called Burt to tell him that Pudge and Kristi had decided against buying the house. Even Miss Adelaide had scurried under the bed when Helen burst into tears after her conversation with Pudge. But she tried not to reveal the depth of her disappointment when she told Burt she was "going out there, see Dad, and list the house. I need to get it settled once and for all."

As she scrunched into the window seat she'd been able to secure on the Southwest plane, she watched as LaGuardia and Manhattan shrank and the snow-patched Pennsylvania landscape that looked like moldy bread came into view. She used to love to fly but vowed to herself she'd go business class the next time. All she was asking was a little more attention. And a lot more space.

Squirming as she tried to get comfortable, she opened a magazine and turned to an article by Reva O'Rourke. Because Reva frequently contributed to *The Arch,* Helen liked to read her work in other publications. But Lord, she thought, Reva's gone off the deep end this time and cranked out a love letter to kale. When, she wondered, had the world started revolving around kale? She hated it in every form.

Disgusted after she'd scanned the first few lines, she thumbed through the rest of the magazine, pausing at features on creative ways to use leftovers from the holidays, the many faces of bed and breakfasts across the country, and imaginative approaches to reducing clutter. Bored with its offerings, she tucked it into the pocket of the seat in front of her.

As she studied the frozen farmland below, she felt the familiar fingers of fear grip her again. Two things were certain: She'd have to rent a car, and she'd have to drive in wintry conditions from Midway to Rockwell at the same time of year as her accident last February. That's okay, she assured herself. That's why I'm taking a morning flight—so I don't need to drive at night. She promised Burt she wouldn't even get behind the wheel of her rental car in Rockwell after sundown.

Closing her eyes, she distracted herself by letting her mind skim the articles she'd seen in the magazine. She had no use for Reva's glowing report on kale but might try some of the tips on de-cluttering. And maybe—if she was lucky—she could convince Burt to spend a few days at a B&B the following summer. She'd always wanted to see what Door County in Wisconsin had to offer.

Although the outside temperature on the dashboard read ten above zero, I-57 was clear of snow patches. Her rental Camry had none of the lumbering road presence she'd always enjoyed with "Black Beauty," but it did possess a certain amount of zip and assertiveness. She appreciated that. Relieved she'd had no encounters with slush or ice, she stopped at McDonald's on the edge of Rockwell to pick up a burger and fries. She was in no mood for banter at The Boulder. After she parked the car in her freshly plowed driveway, she entered her old home.

Thank God for Pudge, she thought. He may not want to buy the house, but he still remembered to scoop off the snow and turn up the thermostat. Almost by reflex, she opened the door of the fridge and found a quart of milk. A box containing two muffins and a pound bag of freshly ground coffee sat in the middle of the kitchen table.

She smiled, tossed her coat over a chair, and put on a pot of coffee. Indeed, Pudge was a wonder! How could she possibly be angry with him for changing his mind? Disheartened, yes, but never angry. She dug her cell from her purse and punched in his number.

When she heard the reserve in his voice, she knew how much he regretted backing out of their deal. Still, he agreed to come to the house at 9:30 the next morning to discuss any work that needed to be done before she called DeeDee Duley to give her the listing.

Munching on her hamburger, she called Burt to report her safe arrival.

"In for the night, I hope," he observed.

When she chuckled, her anxiety over the wintry drive

from the airport evaporated. Picking at her lukewarm fries, she listened while Burt discussed his day.

"Don't forget to check on Miss Adelaide." She surveyed the few remaining rubbery fries and decided against eating them. "Oh—and I have an idea for next summer." She told him about the article she'd read on the plane and suggested they spend part of their vacation at a B&B. "Maybe Door County."

He made no response.

"You know, in Wisconsin."

Again, there was no reply.

"Burt? Are you there?"

"Yeah . . . yeah, I am. Kind of floored by your idea—"

"It wouldn't have to be a long time. Maybe one or two nights—"

"It's the B&B thing." He didn't give her time to finish.

"I thought you'd take a good B&B over a hotel any time." Confused, she stared at her cell.

"I would. That's the thing." His gravelly voice took on a new timbre—eager with anticipation. "I was thinking on my way home tonight that your house would make a terrific B&B."

"Yeah?" Lord, Burt could get her off track sometimes! "Well . . ." She was in no mood to consider other options. All she wanted now was to get rid of the place. "As if any-one ever wanted to visit Rockwell," she told him. "And who'd want to take on the job of running it?" She paused and answered her own question. "Not me. Lord, not me!"

"I know, I know. It's a crazy thought that crossed my mind. Just forget it."

She sighed, aware that the weight of a long travel day was piling in on her.

"I'm beat, Burt. Pudge's coming over tomorrow morning, then after I talk with him I'll tell DeeDee to get it listed asap." As she cleaned up the remnants of her carry-out order, she was grateful that Pudge had put a fresh trash bag in the wastebasket under the sink. "I'll call you tomorrow. It's going to be an early night for me."

"Get some good zzz's." His voice sounded tender. "Wish I were there to tuck you in."

"Me too." She could almost feel his arms around her. "But I wouldn't be worth much."

The next morning, refreshed in spite of her restless sleep, she made coffee and nibbled on a muffin. That Pudge, she thought; he always thinks of everything.

"Anybody home?"

She jumped at the sound of his voice.

"Pudge." Greeting him in the hall, she saw that he carried a bottle of cream soda. In spite of his grin, she could sense his uneasiness.

Skirting the issue of the aborted sale of the house, she suggested the two of them take a quick tour of the downstairs, the upstairs bedrooms, and the attic to decide the most important things that needed to be done. He whipped out a small notebook and stubby pencil and wrote as they walked. In less than an hour they had covered the house and seated themselves at the kitchen table.

"I'll only be here a few days and need to visit my dad a couple of times. But I'd love to see Kristi too. If she hadn't been so firm with me last winter, I might still be sulking in the hospital bed."

"Could be." He studied an item on his list. "She'd like to see you too but—"

"But she feels bad about the house, right?" In spite of her disappointment with Kristi's change of heart, she still felt sorry for Pudge.

"She cried at night. Scared to death we were getting ourselves in too deep." He used his sleeve to smooth out the circle of moisture that his soda had made on the Formica table.

"Pudge, we're good friends. Sometimes friends and business deals don't mix. I want you to know," she adopted the tone she used when she had to make a point with her staff, "that your friendship means more to me than the sale of this house ever will."

He smiled gratefully. "What'll you do?"

"First thing, I'll list it with DeeDee. When I talked with Burt last night, he had a crazy idea—that the place might make a good bed and breakfast. Nice thought—but who would come? And who would use it?"

Pudge's face paled under his red hair. Setting his bottle on the table, he stared at Helen. She tried to read the expression that swept over his face.

"Are you okay?" She wondered if he might be coming down with something.

"Yeah. Yeah." He shook his head. "You're right. That is one crazy idea. But get this—me'n Kristi were talking a few days ago that Rockwell needs a place for people to stay when they come to town."

"But who—"

"Goll-dern! You probably haven't heard that a company's going into the old Midwest building—one that makes ingredients for healthy foods. Cereal, ice cream, stuff like that." The color returned to his face. "Some legal red tape to get through, but it's pretty much a done deal. The guy in charge told me himself." His expression brightened. "There'll be jobs in Rockwell and people coming to town."

"Maybe DeeDee can sell it to one of their managers." Helen began to think aloud. "Or maybe—maybe Burt didn't have such a harebrained idea after all. You know, Pudge, it really could be a wonderful B&B. I'll run that by DeeDee."

Pudge grew thoughtful. Silently, they considered the impact that the new plant would make on the town. After several moments, he spoke first.

"Or maybe—maybe you shouldn't talk to DeeDee. Not yet anyway. Talk to me'n Kristi again first. Please? As a friend?"

Puzzled, she stared at him.

"Let's do this," she suggested. "I'll go see Dad this afternoon. Then let's get a carry-out from The Boulder tonight and have a good visit right here. As friends."

"Tell you what. You call in your order and we'll pick it up along with ours. That way, you don't have to drive at night."

"That'll make Burt happy." She smiled as he pulled on his stocking cap. "Deal."

She closed the door behind him and studied DeeDee Duley's business card. Speculating on what Pudge might want to discuss, she dropped the card back in her purse. She'd wait and call DeeDee tomorrow.

"Stuffed green peppers?"

Helen greeted Pudge and Kristi with a question as they walked through her front door.

"Sorry. I know you ordered a burger, but this was the special," Pudge apologized.

"And it's one of The Boulder's best," Kristi explained. "Oh, Helen, it's great to see you. And look at the way you're getting around—like the accident never happened."

"Believe me, I know it did. Especially during a cold spell, when I ache all over." Helen led them to the kitchen table, where they sat as a family. Realizing something was missing, she popped up and opened a cupboard. Kristi had always enjoyed a glass of something soothing during her visits last winter and nodded when Helen held up a bottle of red wine.

As they attacked the peppers, homemade coleslaw, and crescent rolls, she wondered why people in New York couldn't cook like this. Companionably, the three swapped family updates. Helen told them her dad had seemed more alert that afternoon, while Kristi shared her pride in how well Jenna was juggling her nursing school challenges in Chicago. Mason and his bride were redoing Pudge's mom's house and "happy as—oh, I don't know. What do they say? Clams, that's it. Happy as clams." Kristi held up her glass for a refill.

"Yeah, I'd be happy as a clam too if I could sell this house to someone who loves it as much as you do." There. Helen hoped she hadn't been too blunt but felt she needed to address the obvious.

"Hey, I know." Kristi tipped her glass and giggled. "How about this? You keep the house and turn it into a B&B. Then Pudge and me? We'll run it." A mischievous grin spread across her face as she snickered at her own joke.

Helen and Pudge chuckled, then became quiet.

"Hey, honey, enough of the wine." Pudge shot his wife a straight look.

Helen watched as Kristi returned his comment with the resentful glare of a rebellious child.

"Good dinner." Pudge tried to break the uneasy silence.

"Good wine too." Kristi drained her glass.

"And especially good company." Helen began to relax as the tension broke among them. "I still can't believe it. I used to hate coming back here. Too many bad memories." She shuddered. "But after the accident, all of you helped more than you'll ever know. That's when my old home began to grow on me. Of course," she smiled at Pudge, "all your work has turned it into a different place."

Pudge face reddened.

"And now," she continued, "I've fallen in love. With my own house. Go figure."

"You really don't want to sell it, do you?" Pudge was able to speak the words that she couldn't.

"Only to the two of you. And we all know that's not going to work," she admitted. "So what do we do?" She glanced around the table. "I can't move back to Rockwell but I can't just let the thing stand like this."

"We could, you know." Kristi whispered.

"Could what?" Helen wondered what this delightful friend had up her sleeve.

"What I said." Kristi's words were measured.

Helen reflected on the silly suggestion that Kristi had tossed out during a giddy moment. "Okay, tell us," she urged. "We're listening."

Kristi's expression begged for reassurance. Once she realized Pudge and Helen wanted to hear her thoughts, she took off like a runaway truck racing down a mountain. "This is something I've wondered about doing. I mean, we're at a good time in our lives—Pudge and me. No kids at home but not enough money to buy a place. And you—you've got a place but probably wouldn't want to run a B&B." She paused for a breath. "Would you?"

"No way in hell," Helen agreed.

"So . . ." Kristi was thinking out loud. ". . . If you hold onto the house and Pudge and me run a B&B here, we could all have what we want. Right?"

"Kristi, you're way off base." Although Pudge scolded his wife, Helen had the feeling he might have heard this idea before.

Glancing from Pudge to Kristi and back to Pudge, Helen began to calculate. Right now she was carrying the house financially—a burden, to be sure. Could she possibly arrange things so that the house might generate some money? How many rooms could they rent? What legal hoops would they have to jump through?

"Maybe she's not, Pudge," Helen said. "Maybe not. I

thought I'd call DeeDee tomorrow, but I think I'll hold off. Let's sleep on this and get together tomorrow afternoon. Right here." She held up the nearly empty wine bottle and winked at Kristi. "More?"

"Not tonight." Kristi smile was full and confident—and sober. "Another time maybe."

When the three met the next day at the house, however, it was not to discuss Kristi's idea. Helen had been awakened at 6:30 that morning with a call from an aide at Happy Haven. Her dad had died in his sleep.

Numbly Helen walked through the house, trying to process the news. "Dad died. In his sleep," she repeated as she made the rounds of all the downstairs rooms. Never had she felt so alone, so abandoned. She'd known this moment would come. But now that she was in the middle of it, she was uncertain what to do first. She knew she should notify Haley immediately but decided to call Pudge.

"We went through this with my mom not too long ago." Pudge's voice broke. "We'll be over in a little while, and—and we'll be there for you through the whole thing. You can count on me 'n Kristi."

Before she had a chance to call Haley she heard from Doris Lochschmidt, who volunteered help with anything in the food department.

"I knew your dad from way back," Doris reminded her. "He was a great guy."

For Haley, their dad's passing was a non-event. She said

there was no way she could make the trip from Colorado in the next few days and instructed Helen to put her name on some flowers.

"You always were his favorite anyway." Haley's parting shot scored none of its intended sting. Helen knew that for once her twin sister was right. Stunned, she put down the phone. She was going to have to handle everything herself. Alone.

She soon learned, however, how wrong she'd been to fear she'd have to go through her father's funeral by herself. Once she talked with Pudge and Doris, the stream of assistance overwhelmed her. Her greatest relief came when the funeral director called to say he picked up Mr. Hamilton, and that her dad had made all the arrangements when her mother died.

At times that day she felt like a mere shadow moving through the whirlwind of activity as her "Rockwell family" went into action.

Kristi answered the barrage of phone calls.

Pudge went to the store to buy essentials to get her through the next week.

When Doug, Maria, and Cherisse stopped in, Doug offered to drive her to Happy Haven to get her dad's things. Maria and Cherisse volunteered to sort through a pile of yearbooks and photo albums to find pictures the funeral home could use for a video of his life.

As the last pink rays of winter sun streaked the sky and a chill settled over the house, Doris appeared with sloppy joes, salad, and brownies.

Depleted, Helen sank onto one of the kitchen chairs and

motioned for Doris, Pudge, and Kristi to join her.

"Thought your dad had perked up lately," Doris observed ruefully. "When I saw him a couple of days ago, I talked to him about the old days and how snobby us Sweet Briar kids thought him and the Longworth kids was. He just gave me that grin of his."

Helen reflected on her visit with him the day before. "Yesterday he was the best that I'd seen him in a long time," she said. "The aide warned me about it. Called it 'fatal recovery' when a person has one last burst of energy right before death. I thought she was making that up."

"Seen that a lot of times." Doris nodded. "Guess I'm goin' to be around awhile then cause I haven't had no burst of energy."

For the first time that day, Helen chuckled. She watched Pudge help himself to another sloppy joe and was grateful these dear people were with her. Burt had called earlier to tell her he found a flight to Midway the next morning, and Pudge said he'd drive to Chicago to pick him up.

During her dad's visitation she couldn't believe the number of stories she heard. Strangers and people she hadn't seen in years told her of the ways Walt Hamilton had helped them. Old friends laughed at the pictures of Walt as a seventh-grade Longworth student and a member of the freshman class at Rockwell High.

"That's you standing right in front of him, Miss D." Pudge exploded with laughter, then covered his mouth self-consciously. "Derned if that isn't you!"

"Don't be shootin' your mouth off, Pudge." Doris chided him gently as she studied the picture. "Look—I'm wearin' a skirt and sweater that I bought with money I earned workin' at the truck stop."

Helen made a mental note to thank Maria and Cherisse for selecting pictures that had the power to rekindle the friendships these Rockwell residents had shared for so many years.

Pudge

"I sure wish Kristi wouldn't act so goofy when she gets a little wine in her." Pudge felt he could unload on Burt as the two traveled to Midway the day after the funeral. "She's got Helen all worked up over this B&B thing while she's still upset over losing her dad." He eased into the left lane to pass a semi. "Helen don't need this right now."

"Ordinarily I'd agree with you, but I actually think it's a good diversion." When Burt shifted his weight to be more comfortable, Pudge wished he had a decent car to drive to the airport. Helen and Burt weren't used to trucks with bouncy rides.

"No way." He braked to let a silver Lexus SUV slide in front of him. The guy was going to make his own space whether Pudge gave him room or not.

"Well, think about it for a minute. These last few days have been hard on Helen. Would've been worse if Haley had decided to show," Burt added. "But when we talked about the future of the house, she turned into her old self again. Decisive. Strategic. In charge. That's my girl!"

"Gotta admit you're right." Pudge realized he was playing his cards close to his chest 'cause he didn't want Burt to see how desperately he wanted to live in the Hamilton house with Kristi. He knew in his heart the two of them could fix it up so people would love to stay there.

"You think it's more'n a pipe dream? Jiminy!" He turned on his wipers to move off the slush that a semi splattered all over his windshield. "I mean seriously. Give me an honest answer."

"I wish I knew. One thing I've noticed, Pudge, is that ownership of the house seems to scare the hell out of everyone. Helen thinks she can't afford to keep it forever, and you and Kristi think you can't afford the debt load." He paused. "Unless—"

Swerving to avoid a piece of road kill, Pudge asked, "Unless what?"

"I did some research yesterday and think there are a couple of options. One would be for Helen to retain ownership and be the sole proprietor of a B&B with you and Kristi running the place as her agents. The other would be for the two of you to reconsider a land contract, take possession of the house, and do whatever you wanted with it."

Pudge was so distracted by the two choices that he almost missed his exit to Cicero Avenue. "I had a buddy at Midwest who got stung on one of those," he recalled. "Made his payments right up to the last three, then had a wreck and couldn't work. He'd paid all that money and the owner still kept the house."

"That's sure one of the risks," Burt agreed. "But both you and I know Helen isn't going to be a hard-ass seller. Let me look into the B&B thing for you so you and Kristi can decide if this really can be more than a pipe dream."

Pudge found it hard to focus on his driving while Burt rattled on about stuff he just plain didn't understand. But as he dropped Burt off at the Southwest departure door, he couldn't help but admit it wasn't a bad thing to have a New York lawyer on your side. Not a bad thing at all.

Later that afternoon, back in Rockwell, he decided to stop in at Helen's house and check on her.

"Anybody home?" he called.

"Upstairs," came her muffled reply.

He took the steps two at a time and found her sitting on the floor in her dad's room, surrounded by music albums, the old vinyl kind, he realized. A puffy-faced Helen made no attempt to cover her tears as a beautiful song poured from the record player.

"It's—it's the Carousel Waltz," she sniffled.

"Sure is pretty." Dodging the albums scattered about the room, he sat beside her on the floor. He wished he knew more about other kinds of music. If she'd been playing a good ol' country song, he'd have recognized it right off.

"Mom and Dad used to love to go to Chicago to see musicals." She dabbed her eyes. "They took Haley and me, then they didn't like the newer shows. Said they were too noisy and political."

"Was this one of his favorites?"

Dang! He wondered what he said that made her start blubbering. She'd been so calm at the funeral home when friends came to pay their respects. And at the service and afterward she'd held it together. Never even shed a tear at the cemetery. And now he felt helpless while she sobbed beside him.

"His and mine. Together." She stopped again to let the tears fall freely.

He wished he knew what to do, what to say. Instead, he sat beside her quietly and listened.

"When I was in grade school, he and I used to dance to this," she said. "Mother would make a face and tell us not to break the furniture. Haley'd see us and move her finger in circles around her head, as if she was sure we were cuckoo."

"Sounds like fun." His eyes felt moist as he pictured her back then—large, lumpy Helen having the time of her life with her dad.

"I thought it would cheer me up to listen to these songs," she sputtered. "But when this one came on, I lost it. My dad and I—we'll never—"

He remembered how tough it was for him to hear Nashville sounds after his mom died. They hurt him inside—hurt something fierce 'cause they reminded him of his mother.

"Sorry," she whimpered.

"Got any coffee left?" He couldn't believe he asked her about the drink he couldn't stand. "I could warm it up, and we could have a couple of those cookies from the other day."

"Oh, Pudge, you really know how to treat a girl." She stood on shaky legs and steadied herself by the bedpost. "You don't want coffee though—"

"Got me a soda out in the truck."

It was good to see her show a hint of a smile, he thought as he hurried down the stairs. He couldn't bother her right now with thoughts about the future of the house.

Monty

Mid-March

"**L**ots of room for expansion. When we need it."
Strunke gazed at the vast production area. "That's a good thing."

Monty breathed a sigh of relief. He had worried that his boss might think the old Midwest plant was too spacious.

"Those offices will have to be gutted and updated though." Strunke fiddled with his ear lobe. "Nobody's going to want to spend their day in cramped cubicles like those."

"Couldn't agree more." Al chimed in.

Monty thought he heard a noise in the front entrance and went to check.

"Anybody home?"

"Hey, Pudge. You had me scared for a minute." He grasped the extended rough hand.

"Sorry 'bout that. Seen your car and thought I'd stop and say hi. Everything going okay?"

"Pretty much on schedule to open in July, we think. We hope. Got the boss and Al—you remember him—with me today. We're figuring out how we want to use the space."

Monty paused, realizing the huge volume of the building's history lodged in this guy's head. "Come on back. Walk with us. Tell us how it used to be."

Pudge hesitated. "'Fraid I'd slow you down. I'll be on my way."

Monty persisted and promised they'd keep him no longer than ten minutes. Pudge was one of those diamond-in-the-rough workers who knew more about production than the front office ever would. But if Pudge felt shy and reluctant about spending time with Strunke and Al, he never showed it.

Grinning, he shook hands with them and motioned toward the empty production area.

"Spent most of my life in here," he said.

Strunke appeared fascinated, while Al kept sneaking peeks at his cell phone. Monty listened as Pudge explained that he'd started working there as a teen, sweeping up and keeping the space clean. "Thought I was pretty big stuff," Pudge admitted.

He then explained how different sections of the vast space had been used over the years. He shared with them his own saga of rising from a machine operator to inspector and finally to line foreman.

"Midwest was good to us—sent us to training classes, cared for our families." He shook his head. "But things wasn't the same after it was sold. Still, we never thought the owners'd clear out and leave all of us with nuthin'." He shuffled his feet. "Just nuthin'."

"You think you'll put in an application?" Although

Strunke fired the question straight at him, Pudge turned and glanced around as if the bigwig might be talking to someone else.

"Who—me?"

"We're going to start taking applications in about a month," Al answered.

"What would I do?" Pudge wondered. "I'm a decent handyman but—"

"You never can tell." Monty was beginning to see Pudge in a different light.

"Watch for the sign to go up in about three weeks. Then pick up an application and see what you think."

"Guess I've nuthin' to lose."

Monty escorted Pudge to the door and watched as he climbed into his old pickup. As he returned to the work area he heard Strunke comment, "You know, I like that guy."

Pudge

April

Two weeks after he'd taken Strunke and Cooper on the tour of the Midwest building, he couldn't shake the sadness that crept into his bones. He yearned for his old job at the factory but guessed he'd pick up an application for the new plant when the time came. It couldn't hurt anything. And the longing he carried around with him to move into Helen's house and make Kristi happy hounded him constantly.

"You sure are in a funk, you know that?" Kristi frowned at him as they ate supper. "You'd think somebody died or somethin'."

"Somebody did a while back. Helen's dad." There. That might get him off the hook. He was giving his wife an "I-don't-want-to-talk-about-it" look when the phone rang.

They never watched a minute of "Wheel of Fortune"

that night. As they listened to Helen's voice on the speaker phone, they were stunned by her latest plan.

"I don't want anyone else in my house. You two love it. You should be there." She took a deep breath. "Look—we can make this happen. I have half my dad's estate so now I can afford to rent you the house for a minimum amount. Later we can talk about a land contract or explore the idea of developing it into a B&B."

Pudge was too shocked to respond.

"If it's okay with the two of you, I'll have Burt draw up an agreement we can all sign. I do have one request, and I'm serious about it: Bring some life back into the place."

Five days later, Pudge, his brother Roy, Mason, and a couple of guys from the old Midwest crew loaded furniture and took it to the Hamilton house.

"Think this place'll be big enough?" Roy cracked. "Hell, we could move the whole Simpkins clan in here and still have room left over."

Kristi zipped through the house, humming as she transferred kitchen utensils from cartons to cupboards and put old but clean sheets on their bed.

"You're higher'n a kite, Kristi," Pudge observed with a smile. "Don't come down too soon or too fast."

The following week, as he spread paint on the front door of Doug's latest rehab, he found himself back in the wishing mode. This time he wished he hadn't given his wife those instructions about coming down from her high too soon. Kristi continued to remain wound up "tighter'n an eight-day clock," as his mom used to say.

Dipping his brush in the sage green paint, he worked

carefully around the door area. He knew Kristi and him would always be grateful to Helen for making it possible for them to live in the house. But now he was getting as antsy as his wife. Too much happening too fast. On the raw and rainy morning when they moved, they even struck a deal to sell their old house to one of Mason's friends.

"Goll-dern it!" He'd let his hand get shaky and smudged paint on the siding. He grabbed a rag and cleaned it off, disgusted that he let his thoughts get the best of him.

Trying to remain positive, he made himself focus on the future. That's what his mom had always taught when he got the heebie-jeebies. He guessed he'd pick up an application for work on one of the new production lines when GRN was ready to hire. After all, a steady job would sure go a long way toward making their monthly payments to Helen. If he could land a spot in the factory—and if he, Kristi, and Helen could handle all the legal hurdles required to open a B&B— he'd be a happy man.

But that was another thing. Earlier in the week, when Kristi and him found themselves tangled up in B&B forms and red tape, he'd called Burt for help. Burt explained that although Helen would be listed as the sole proprietor of "Hamilton House," Pudge and Kristi, acting as her agents, would need to take an exam and submit a floor plan to the Rockwell Fire Department.

That had sure set Kristi off!

"I've never been good at taking tests," she protested. "Not in my whole life!"

"Me neither," he admitted.

The real kicker came the day before when they learned

the outlandish insurance premium Helen would have to pay.

"I don't want to burst your bubble," Helen grumbled on the phone that night, "but I'm not sure our little B&B is going to be worth that kind of overhead."

Jiminy, he thought, I hope we haven't made the biggest mistake of our lives. Once again, he left a glob of green on the new front door Doug had installed the day before.

"Dern it to hell! Might as well quit for the day."

He'd go sit in his truck for a few minutes and guzzle a soda. Might settle his nerves.

A week later, still feeling the willies churning in his gut as he drove through Rockwell, he decided to bypass The Boulder and go straight to the GRN building. Gordon Strunke had called to tell him that he'd reviewed his work application and that there were "some things he needed to talk to him about."

Pudge hoped this job application thing wasn't about to get as crazy complicated as the requirements for a B&B. Was Strunke going to let him down easy, tell him he wasn't going to fit in at the new plant? Whatever the reason, Pudge didn't want to keep the big boss waiting.

As he parked his pickup in the factory lot, he couldn't help but remember how many times he'd done this before when he was a kid. Swinging his lunch bucket and going through these very doors had been part of his daily routine for more years than he cared to add up. However, when he stepped inside and saw the changes in the old building, he stopped dead in his tracks. Gray cement block walls had been covered with a sunny yellow, while the machines installed for the assembly lines were decked out in red, blue, green, and bright orange.

Grinning as he sniffed the combined odors of dry wall, fresh paint, and hot metal, he headed for the cubicle Strunke had claimed as his temporary office.

"Am I in the right place?" he asked as he shook hands with Strunke. "Sure looks different."

"There's no reason why working on an assembly line can't be fun," Strunke replied, motioning for Pudge to sit in front of his desk. He grew serious. "That's what I wanted to talk with you about."

Pudge blinked hard so tears wouldn't show how upset he was. There wasn't going to be a place for him here after all. His head felt fuzzy inside as he tried to concentrate on Strunke's words.

"Reviewed your application . . .wanted to tell you in person that I don't think you're right for the line here."

Pudge nodded numbly. Kristi was going to be crushed.

"Maybe fifteen years ago when you were younger . . ."

Pudge clenched his teeth. He wasn't <u>that</u> old!

"But you've been a line foreman at Midwest, right?"

Pudge nodded.

"I talked with Monty and Al about that, and they agree you'd be the right man as general foreman over all the lines. That is if you'd consider it."

"Wha—" Any words he could find stuck in his throat.

"You've got experience. And you're local. You know the people we're going to hire. That's important. Real important."

Pudge took a deep breath and tried to listen while Strunke droned on about the culture of GRN. He perked up when Strunke rattled off the specifics—salary (more than double what he made at Midwest) and benefits (his head was starting to swim). "Think you'd be interested?"

Pudge thought he might fall off the chair. Interested? Goll-dern, this was beyond his wildest dreams! "You bet."

"Human Resources will be here next week to interview line workers," Strunke said. "They can fill you in on benefits and all."

Pudge's legs wobbled as he followed Strunke through the plant and heard how the space would be used. He tried to keep it all together as he thanked his new boss, left the building, and fired up his truck. Still in control of his emotions, he cruised through town and passed The Boulder. It was only when he went out of his way and drove by his mom's old house that he finally allowed the tears of gratitude to stream down his face.

He thought he'd wait until after supper to tell Kristi about his job, but when she gave him that questioning look as he came through the back door, he couldn't keep his news bottled up. For the first time in months, he saw the smile that he'd fallen in love with light up her face.

"Omigod!" She dropped the spoon in the skillet and ran to hug him. "Omigod!"

He thought he could stand here forever with her arms around him and the peppery aroma from her sausage gravy tickling his nose. He was home, in their dream home, and he had a job. A real job!

They ate a supper that never tasted so good while Pudge poured out all the information Strunke had given him.

"I'm so proud, so damn proud." Kristi smiled and shook her head in wonder.

Suddenly famished, he got up, grabbed another biscuit, and smothered it with sausage gravy.

"I talked with Jenna while you were out." Kristi began to clear the table while he devoured his second helping. "She's coming home next weekend. Said she wants to help us get settled in."

"We've pretty much done that already." He eyed the plate of chocolate chip cookies she placed down in front of him. "But it'll sure be nice to have her home."

"I've gotta tell you," Kristi sat down and took a bite from a cookie. "I did mention to her—casually, mind you—that I've been kinda upset about all the fees and regulations of running a B&B. I can't believe the amount of red tape it takes for a few folks to spend a night at a homey place."

"Yeah?" He was surprised Kristi told Jenna how nervous she'd been.

"You'll never guess what she said."

He shrugged and grinned, clueless about their daughter's reaction but enjoying the bright look of expectancy in Kristi's eyes.

" Well—yeah, Jenna said she has a friend in nurses' training whose parents have a house they only offer to people coming through town for a night or two. They aren't registered. They don't advertise. They don't even charge. They rely on friends to send them clients, then ask their guests to pay whatever they'd like."

He reached for a cookie, then decided to take two. "No kidding?"

"No kidding," she said. "And go on and eat all the cookies you want."

"Dern." He grinned. "That'd sure take the pressure off. Wouldn't it?"

Monty

August

He could hardly believe almost two years had passed since he and Al had made their first trip along this road. Monty lowered the windows in the Beemer so he could smell the clover as he followed the sliver of patchy state highway that led to Rockwell. He slowed to appreciate the mid-afternoon sun warming the miles of flourishing corn and soybeans. Two years ago he would've considered them part of the landscape of no-man's land.

He remembered how uptight he'd been that first day— hell-bent to move on to Danville to evaluate the town as a possible location site for GRN. He'd been stressed over some meeting he had that night and Theo's need to practice-practice-practice his three-point shooting. That was about the time Claire nagged him to help her find a house in a more prestigious community. God, he thought, he and his family may have appeared ideal, but inside the walls of their home they had simmered in a cauldron of self-created tension.

He drove past the new facility, where construction crews

were fine-tuning the interior. Smiling, he passed The Boulder and thought of the delicious food he'd enjoyed there and the meals still to come. He meandered through residential streets until he found the big home where Pudge and his wife now lived and was grateful they had asked him to spend the night.

"Kristi says she's gotta practice making muffins on someone, and it might as well be you," Pudge joked with him on the phone a few days ago. "You'll be our first guinea pig—I mean guest."

Monty took a moment to study the two-story Queen Anne house at the end of the gently curving sidewalk lined with brilliant marigolds. Then he grabbed his bag and strolled toward the front steps. Pudge had come a long way from his tiny childhood home crammed with red-haired kids. Monty punched the doorbell button and waited.

"You must be Kristi." He stuck out his hand to the solid woman who exuded friendliness as she greeted him. "I'm Monty."

"Oh, I wasn't sure when you were coming. I'm baking a batch of muffins." When she attempted to brush a patch of flour away from her nose, she merely added to it. "We're honored to have you as our first guest."

Stepping inside, he felt surrounded by a genuine warmth that he seldom noticed in the new houses of his friends. Someone must have carefully chosen which items to keep from the previous owner, then blended in Pudge and Kristi's tastes to give the place its flavor. He sighed contentedly as he realized he'd feel at home here.

"Hey, buddy." Pudge was behind him with a clap on the back. "Glad to see you made it."

Kristi scurried to the kitchen, explaining she didn't want to burn the muffins.

"This place? It's a work in progress. That's for dern sure." Pudge gave him a tour of the first floor, then showed him the upstairs bedrooms. Each had a cozy ambiance of its own, Monty noticed, wishing that Claire had come with him. Pudge explained that one room would be kept available for "the great lady who's selling us this place. Helen Hamilton'd like to be able to come home when she feels like it."

"I think I met her at that Comfort Food Day when I brought Al and Strunke to look at the town," Monty recalled. "She and a guy from New York sat across from us."

"That'd be her, all right." Pudge grinned. "We've kinda become like family." He went on to say he'd give Monty "about fifteen minutes" to himself, then they could take the pickup down to the GRN building so Monty could check out the progress. "That is, if you don't mind riding in my truck."

"I'd love it," Monty lied. "Been in my car all afternoon."

He took a few minutes to freshen up and to admire the soft cinnamon-and-cream colors in his room—welcoming but not too fussy. Looking out the window at the surrounding maples and oaks, he spotted one towering oak that would have been the perfect place for a tree house if he and Claire had lived here when their kids were young.

At the plant, he was amazed at the progress during the last few weeks. All traces of Midwest had been hauled away, and the rooms reconfigured for GRN production and offices.

"Had some trouble with one of the contractors getting sick on us. Had to have open-heart surgery, but his Number Two man stepped up." Pudge stopped to examine the seal of a machine that had been set the day before in fresh concrete. "You can tell Strunke we're right on schedule."

"He's a good guy," Monty said. "And he's pumped about this Rockwell project."

When the two of them met Kristi at The Boulder for supper, Monty was pleased he recognized two of the town council members. Between forkfuls of Swiss steak "like my mom used to make" he asked Pudge and Kristi how the townspeople were feeling about GRN.

"DeeDee Duley, our realtor who never sleeps? She's been busier'n a one-armed paper hanger," Pudge replied. "A few families want to move in before school starts next week."

"Pudge!" Kristi shook her head at his choice of words, then added, "Even Doug Lochschmidt has sold one of his rehabbed houses to a fellow. Didn't he say somebody else's interested in another one?"

"Yep—but I don't have time to help him. My nephew— Roy's son—is doing some painting for him." Pudge ran his fork around his plate to collect the rest of his mashed potatoes.

"Sometime I want to bring Claire—that's my wife— to see the plant and, well, the town itself." Monty grinned as the server put down pieces of warm blueberry pie with vanilla ice cream.

"She got a job?" Pudge wondered.

Digging into his pie, Monty stopped to savor its taste. "Umm," he said, "not a real one. But she spends a lot of time at an antique shop that her friend, Sylvia, owns."

Kristi nodded thoughtfully.

"Sylvia's been looking for a location for a second shop—fancies herself as an entrepreneur. You wouldn't believe the amount of old stuff she's collected. It's practically spilling out the doors and windows."

"Sounds like Helen's attic." Pudge snickered.

"Got that right." Kristi poked the air with her fork. "You tell your wife to get her butt down here and bring Sylvia with her. They'd have a ball looking at a couple of empty storefronts."

"One thing I'll never understand about that antique business is how some folks can't get enough of other people's junk." Pudge polished off his last bite of pie. "But Kristi's right. Your wife and her friend oughtta come down here and look."

"And they could stay with us. Wouldn't cost 'em a cent." Kristi's green eyes sparkled at the thought of hosting two women out on a lark.

Monty knew he'd have to mention it to Claire. She and Sylvia might enjoy a day combing the downtown area for a cozy spot for the new store.

When he paid his bill, he asked the young man at the register about Doris.

"Oh, Grando usually goes home early in the afternoon," he replied. "I'm her grandson, Carter. Used to work at McDonald's until I woke up and realized where the best food in Rockwell really is."

"Well, you tell your grandma that Monty is in town and will be in for lunch tomorrow. I'll be busy all morning, but I don't think I could head home without seeing her." When the young man grinned, Monty thought, "That guy's got

Lochschmidt written all over him."

The following morning, fortified by Kristi's scrambled eggs and blueberry muffins, Monty began a series of meetings with team leaders at the plant. Encouraged by the optimism of the new hires, he couldn't wait to give Strunke a glowing report. He had finished his last session when Pudge opened the office door.

"Got a minute?" His face was drawn. "We need to talk."

"Sure." Monty motioned for him to take a chair. "Something wrong?"

"Shoot. I knew it was too good to be true." Pudge's fingers drummed on the table. "I just had a call from one of our major suppliers. Their workers are going on strike today, and they'll be shut down for God-knows-how-long."

"Damn." Monty felt as if he'd been slapped in the face. "Those guys are plain crazy. Why would they shut the door on several weeks of guaranteed work?"

"Don't make no sense." Pudge lapsed into the grammar he'd learned from his hard-working parents. "Guess they think they'll scare management into giving them everything they're askin' for in a new contract."

"Stupid. Strunke's not going to be pleased. And you have yet to see Strunke when he's not pleased." He scooped up his papers and stuffed them into his briefcase. "I'll talk to him on my way back. God, I couldn't wait to tell him how smoothly everything's going. And now this."

Pudge looked like a dog who'd been whipped. "And now this," he echoed.

Doris

October

She didn't think she'd ever had butterflies like this—not when she stood before a Justice of the Peace and married Bill, not when she piled six kids into her old car and left the farm and Bill along with it, not when she sat in a bar in one of New York's fanciest hotels and listened to her brother Tommy play the piano like he'd done when they were growing up in their shabby house on the Sweet Briar side of town.

Today, all she had to do was hold a pair of huge dumb-looking scissors and cut a ribbon. But in front of a humongous crowd standing around the old Midwest plant! She'd have to remember to call it GRN from now on. She squinted into the mid-morning sun that painted the orange and gold leaves on the maple trees across the street so bright she wished she'd worn dark glasses.

As the Rockwell High School band finished playing "America the Beautiful," a long-haired guy from Channel 3 in Champaign swung his camera around and scanned six others lining up with her— their congressman, town council president, Strunke, GRN's new Rockwell general manager, Monty, and Pudge. All men. Why the hell had they asked her? She'd rather be mixing up a meat loaf at The Boulder right now. Doing something sensible.

But that damn Monty and Pudge wouldn't take no for an answer—said there wouldn't be a new GRN plant there if it hadn't been for her. Sweet-talked her by remindin' her that she started the Comfort Food Days that kept the spirits of the local folks from hitting rock bottom during those awful times after Midwest closed.

They'd told her she'd be the perfect one to represent the citizens of Rockwell at the ribbon-cutting. Well, she just hoped the damn citizens of Rockwell out there couldn't see her legs shakin' inside the new black pantsuit she'd bought at Penney's in Champaign. Darcy had driven her over there the week before, and they met her other daughter Debbie for lunch at Applebee's. A real nice day, but she knew The Boulder's food was better.

Shit, she thought as the congressman droned on, what would her old Fearless Four friends think if they could see her now, standing up there with all them bigwigs? Well, not Pudge, she reminded herself; he was a Sweet Briar kid like her who'd worked hard and made good. But Rosie, Kate, and Cheryl would have done something out there in the crowd to distract her and crack her up.

A gentle breeze tickled her nose. For a moment she was afraid she'd sneeze, but all of a sudden Strunke was telling them to get their scissors ready and "1-2-3, Snip." She cut through the ribbon slick as a whistle. Hell, that wasn't so bad after all. She grinned when the townsfolk cheered and let loose hundreds of bright green balloons into the blue October sky. With the band tuning up on "Happy Days Are Here Again," she was tempted to join the kids dancing in the street.

She felt Pudge take her arm and steer her toward the front door.

"Come on, Miss D. You're one of the honored guests to take the first official tour," he shouted above the music.

"You're lookin' pretty sharp," she told him. He seemed at ease in his crisp new khakis and navy blue sport coat. "Hey, I gotta—" She nodded toward the ladies' room.

"First things first." He gave her an understanding smile. "I'll wait."

As she waved her hands under the dryer, she recalled how stressed and washed-out Pudge had looked when he told her the GRN opening might be delayed. Then he came into The Boulder a few days later and reported that Strunke had played a few trump cards and found another company that could supply the necessary materials on time and at a cheaper cost. She learned she liked Strunke better every time she saw him and was glad he made a good deal out of a big mess.

"C'mon, Miss D, I want to show you around. You won't recognize the building."

Damn right, she thought, as Pudge led her through processing areas and packaging lines. It seemed like a happy place, with walls and machines decked out in yellow, red, blue, green and even orange—the colors little Cory might have picked out from his box of crayons.

"Wish my mom coulda seen this." She spoke softly

as she recalled the heavy gray environment of the former Midwest factory where her own mother had toiled for years to keep bread on their table and shoes on their feet.

"Mine too," Pudge agreed. "Whoever would have thought a production plant could look like a kid's playroom?"

"That what they call it now? Not 'factory'?"

"You got it, Miss D. Times has changed."

When they threaded their way through the sparkling new facility, Doris saw Monty waving to her.

"Somebody wants to talk with you," he called.

"I'm about ready to sit down anyway," she answered.

"This is Leslie McDonnell from the *Chicago Tribune*. She wants to ask you about Comfort Food Day."

As Monty escorted them into an available office, Doris studied the young underfed blonde who didn't look much older than Cherisse. "She went to Northwestern. Like me," he assured her.

"And I grew up in a town about this size in northern Indiana," Leslie added.

"Then you can't be all bad." Doris squirmed to get comfortable on the hard chair and grimaced when Monty added that the Channel 3 guy wanted a few minutes with her too. Her new pants suit was starting to feel scratchy, and she was ready to go home and put on her old clothes and slippers.

However, she liked this girl Leslie. She reminded Doris of her old friend Kate, who'd been a newspaper reporter and author. After she told Leslie how the folks in town had been "pretty much whipped by Midwest's decision to shut its plant," she let down her guard and explained all about Comfort Food Day and how everyone needed to get together for "home cookin' and fellowship." By the time the Channel 3 guy shot some film of her talking with Monty and Strunke and interviewed her about how important "good food and plenty of it" was to a person's morale, she felt her energy returning.

"I want both of you to go down to The Boulder and tell 'em Doris said you need a big plate of meat loaf and a piece of pie. It's been real nice talking with you," she told Leslie and the cameraman. "And you come back and see us any time you can."

It's funny, she thought, as she glanced around the new place, two years ago the bottom fell out for most of us. But look at us now—carryin' on 'n celebratin' like we won the lotto. She recalled how her older brother, Charley, had come back with a college degree and several years of experience and taken over the top spot at Midwest. He'd been a good manager for many years and, thank God, retired before the company decided to close the factory in Rockwell. She could see Pudge explaining some of the new equipment to visitors and Monty laughing with Strunke. They'd never miss her if she slipped out now.

Once she was home and changed her clothes, she called Rosie. "You gotta turn on Channel 3 news at 6," she told her old friend. "I might be on but probably not. I talked with one of their guys at the ribbon-cutting today."

Rosie wheezed, as she did so often these days, and told her she'd watch. "But right now I'm busy with my afternoon shows. Catch ya later."

She hung up and wished Cheryl could get Channel 3 in the Chicago area. For the first time in ages, she ached to see

Kate. Maybe bein' with that girl reporter today had made her homesick for her old friend.

Doris sighed. The house was so quiet you could hear the floors creak even when nobody was walkin' on 'em. Grabbing an old cardigan, she went out to sit on the front-porch swing and listened to the shrieks from kids walkin' home from school and the band practicin' on the football field several blocks away. Three robins scuttled through the brown oak leaves in her front yard, then chirped anxiously like they'd better get on their way south. And off they went.

She breathed a sigh of relief when she saw Mallory's car zipping into the driveway. At least someone was home. And the stillness that had seemed so quiet compared to all the hullabaloo at the GRN plant would be replaced by clattering dishes, supper sounds, and Mallory's family jabbering at once.

"Grando!" Mallory called. "We've gotta turn on the TV. Someone said you might be on the news."

She stood and steadied herself on her cane. "Better check it out, I s'pose." She gave Mallory a hug, grateful she still had plenty of activity in the place she'd called home for more than fifty years. "Sure hope I didn't make a damn fool of myself."

Epilogue

November 2014

Cherisse

I am so excited I can hardly write this! In fact, so much has happened lately that I don't know where to begin. But here goes. Miss Helen came for a long weekend to work out some business stuff about her house with Pudge and Kristi. While she was here, she invited me 'n Ruby—I mean Ruby and me. Miss Helen says if I'm going to be a writer, I have to use good English. Anyway, she invited the two of us to come to New York for Thanksgiving! I can't believe it. She said she has some airline credits to use and will buy our tickets. We'll stay on an inflatable mattress in her living room and hope Miss Adelaide doesn't bother us too much. She and Burt will cook the dinner, but she wants Ruby and me—mainly me—to make Grando's sage dressing. That's easy. I've been helping with that since I was old enough to chop with a knife.

We'll go to the Macy's parade, but other than that, Miss Helen said we won't do a lot of "touristy" things. She wants to show us her office and hit some of the funky restaurants in the East and West Village. We'll take the subway uptown and maybe go to the top of the Empire State Building, and she definitely wants us to check out the hotel where Uncle Tommy played the piano for years. This could be even more exciting than seeing Kevin Harvick win at the Brickyard.

Miss Helen plans to come back here and stay in her old room a few times a year. Her and—oops, she and—Pudge 'n Kristi have gotten to be real good friends. I know they helped her a lot after she had that awful wreck, and they're pretty tight now that they're living in her house. I don't quite get their arrangement, but whatever it is seems to work.

Their bedrooms are full every weekend when the U of I has a home game. That guy Strunke, who's some sort of bigwig with GRN, stays there when he comes to the games. Sometimes he brings other people to see the new plant during the week.

The other guy from GRN—his name is Monty—still comes to town, mainly to eat French toast at The Boulder, I think. I overheard him telling Pudge when I wiped off the table at the booth next to theirs that, "I thought I had made sure Strunke met the important people in town, but it was that straggly kid who has to repeat third grade who really sold him. Who would have thought?"

Then I pretended to scrape some syrup off the table so I could hear what he said next. He told Pudge that he and his wife are flying to New York in the spring to see their son dance in a big ballet at a place called "Purchase." I think that must be his college. He said it's near the city.

You know, you can hear a lot of news if you clean tables real slow when the people next to you are talking. Grando taught me that trick.

I still can't believe the commotion she stirred up when she talked with those reporters last month. Everybody in town said she was the star of Channel 3 news that night. Then— can you believe it—*USA Today* picked up the story from the one in the Chicago paper and came to talk to Grando. The reporter and photographer ate with her at The Boulder when they were here. Thank God all this attention hasn't caused her to forget how to make my favorite Polish dinner!

Someday I think I'd like to go to college and learn how to write real good—real well. I'd like to do articles about food. I know people's tastes change, like right now everybody's big on kale and quinoa. But I want to make sure they all remember the kind of food Grando makes. She calls it "Comfort Food" and says it feeds the soul as well as the body.

Like she always tells me, "When it comes from the heart and you add a little love, it always turns out good."

CPSIA information can be obtained
at www.ICGtesting.com
Printed in the USA
LVHW011241290620
659168LV00002B/199